Elves of the Arctic
A Christmas Encounter

S J WOODWARD

For Belle, the best writing and Christmas companion anyone could ever wish for.
And for my wonderful mum, who gave me her Christmas spirit.

CONTENTS

In a land of snow and frosty might,
Where Northern lights dance in skies so bright.
Dwell magical folk, both merry and old,
The North Pole Elves, their stories untold.

Crafting toys for Santa's sleigh,
To bring joy to the world on Christmas Day.
Their hands work hard with skill and care,
Creating wonders beyond compare,
Dolls that dance and trains that sing,
Enchantment to all they gladly bring.

Guiding the sleigh through the night,
A shimmering trail of pure starlight.
But elves are more than just a few,
They teach us lessons, old and true,
To cherish, to love, to give, to share,
To show kindness and friendship everywhere.

So, remember the elves of North Pole's cold,
With hearts so pure and spirits bold,
In the season of wonder, let their story be told,
The Elves of the Arctic, in legends of old.

- CHAPTER ONE -

GREENLAND

The journey from London to Greenland was long, but the view from the plane was worth every second. High above the Arctic Ocean with huge chunks of ice floating below and snow-covered mountains in the distance. It was like something out of a dream.

This adventure had taken the Brown Family first through Iceland, where Poppy's dad, Mr Brown, took the chance to meet up with some old work friends in Reykjavik. He worked for a sporting goods company and had a knack for making friends wherever he went. Poppy and her brother, Jack, were used to these stop-offs to visit people they called "aunts" and "uncles," even though they weren't related.

Poppy was fine with the detour; it was just a quick stop on their way to a much bigger adventure.

Mr Brown was a thrill-seeker, and he had an action-packed few days planned for them in Greenland: dog sledding, ice fishing, and kayaking, before returning home for Christmas Day. It was a trip the family had always dreamed of taking together.

Mr Brown and Jack loved kayaking; they'd often spend their weekends exploring the beautiful rivers of the Norfolk Broads at Poppy's grandparents' house.

Poppy, on the other hand, was far more comfortable on land with her nose in a good book - she was excited about this trip, though, especially the dog sledding part. Mr. Brown had been talking about it for months, sharing facts with them like he was a tour guide for Greenland. Jack was just as excited.

"Poppy, did you know that every year in Greenland, the sun doesn't set for two months? Imagine not having to go to bed or get up for school for two months!" he said, interrupting her thoughts. She looked at him...was he joking?

"Look! I think we're nearly there!" she said, changing the subject. They both leaned over to get a closer look out the window and sure enough, they were rapidly approaching the frozen coastline.

"Poppy, Jack, make sure you've got everything," called Mrs Brown from the seats in front as she struggled with her overflowing backpack. "We can't get back on the plane if we forget anything - Dad's got your coats here."

Poppy really liked her new red coat. In fact, the whole family had gotten new coats for the trip. Mr Brown and Jack decided to match in bright orange (Mr Brown's favourite colour), while Mrs Brown chose a bright blue coat with a green zip. There was no way they'd be losing each other in the airport!

The freezing air hit their faces as they approached the front of the plane, and Poppy felt extra thankful for all her layers.

The airport was small, and the staff were bundled up in thick coats and fluffy hats. After showing their passports, they found the pickup spot where a small bus was waiting for them.

The roads were uneven and icy - it was like riding in a bumper car! Thankfully, they soon arrived at the hotel - a long, red building with tall windows and a beautiful view of the crystal bay below.

"Welcome to your hotel. We hope you have a fantastic stay with us," said the cheerful driver.

Inside the hotel lobby was a roaring log fire with comfy armchairs, and several families were already sprawled out, relaxing and playing board games.

"Aluu, welcome to Greenland," said the lady at the reception.

"Aluu, thank you very much. We're excited to be here," said Mr Brown, obviously proud to have learned the word "Aluu," which Poppy guessed meant 'Hello' in Greenlandic. "Brown family checking in, please."

Their rooms were up on the third floor. Jack rushed ahead to check them out, hoping to get the best one, but the rooms were pretty much the same. Both had a floor-to-ceiling window with a bench seat that looked out on the bay. Poppy imagined herself sitting there in the evenings with a book. The rest of the room was simple and neat, very different from Poppy's room back at home, which was jam-packed with posters, board games, video games, and a ton of books.

Everyone was exhausted - they decided to order room-service pizza for dinner and head to bed.

As Poppy stood brushing her teeth, her mind buzzed with excitement for the adventures waiting for them the next day.

"Night, Jack," she whispered as she climbed into bed.

"Sleep tight," he replied, already half asleep.

- CHAPTER TWO -

DOG SLEDDING

Poppy felt completely refreshed after a good night's sleep. She could already hear her parents shuffling around next door.

"Poppy! Jack! Come to our room when you're ready. We've ordered breakfast here to save time; it won't be long." called Mrs Brown.

Everyone was in good spirits this morning. A proper sit-down family breakfast was a rare treat for the Browns, as Mrs Brown worked nights at the hospital. Usually, breakfast consisted of Mr Brown throwing toast at Poppy and Jack as they rushed out the door on their way to school.

They finished eating and started getting ready, which, in true Brown family style, was a complete disaster.

No one had unpacked anything the night before, so all their belongings were either buried at the bottom of their bags or mixed up with someone else's.

By the time they were ready to go, it looked like a small tornado had swept through both rooms. Mrs Brown attempted to pick up a few items from the floor to spare the housekeeping staff, but it was hopeless… and they were late.

They rushed down to the meeting point where the bus was, thankfully, still waiting for them.

It was a different driver today, a woman with short blonde hair and a strict face who barked at them to get on board quickly.

Mrs Brown was flustered; she hated being late for things. Poppy saw her offering apologetic waves to the others already on board as they took their seats at the front.

The driver seemed to calm down once they got on the road, chatting to Mr and Mrs Brown about kayaking in the local area.

Soon, they arrived at the dog sledding centre, and their guide, Malik, gave them a safety briefing and told them more about the history of dog sledding in Greenland. Poppy was more excited than ever to get started, and Jack looked like he might explode.

Heading outside to meet the mushers and dogs, they took the opportunity for some photos. A topic which had caused some disagreement earlier this morning.

Poppy had wanted to bring her phone to take pictures, but Mr Brown had imposed a strict "no phone" policy outside of the hotel, fearing that they (which she knew meant Jack) would lose them.

The Huskies were stunning, with thick white and copper coats and piercing blue eyes. Poppy couldn't believe how loud they were! Their excited barks filled the air - they were ready to go!

Mr and Mrs Brown boarded the first sled while Poppy and Jack climbed into the second. Poppy was pleasantly surprised by how comfortable and roomy it was and immediately wrapped herself in some of the blankets.

"Jack, give your bag to Poppy to keep in the back," Mrs Brown shouted from the front sled.

Poppy couldn't help but roll her eyes at this request. Jack was only eighteen months younger, but their parents often forgot this and treated him like a baby (a fact that he cleverly used to his advantage on many occasions). Once everyone was settled, the mushers conducted their final checks, and they set off.

The feeling of being pulled along on the sled was like nothing else. The dogs were so well trained, working in perfect harmony as their powerful paws pounded on the ice below.

As they sped up, Poppy sat back to enjoy the incredible scenery surrounding them. Everything was so beautiful. Up ahead, she could see her parents, their arms wrapped around each other, enjoying the ride.

Mr and Mrs Brown had been together for many years but only married for five. Not for any particular reason, they would say, just because they'd never gotten round to it, which Poppy could completely believe. Her parents were wonderful, fun, incredible people - but organisation was definitely not their strong suit.

After some time, the wind picked up a lot, and snow began falling so hard they could barely see.

Poppy buried her face in her scarf as she reached for an extra blanket to shield Jack from the snow, pelting him head-on.

"We're heading for the trees over there until this blizzard passes," the musher called out. "Your parents are going that way too; we'll catch them up."

But as the dogs guided them towards the trees, a terrifying sight appeared.

A herd of about twenty Musk Oxen, resembling woolly mammoths, emerged from the trees and began charging in their direction. Startled by the first sled and trying to protect their young.

Suddenly, everything started to move in slow motion. The dogs at the front spotted the herd and became frantic, turning in the opposite direction to the rest of the pack.

This caused the sled to tip sharply on its edge, and Poppy and Jack watched in horror as the musher lost her grip and was thrown into the snow.

Poppy tried to see if she was hurt, but she was rapidly disappearing from view, and with the sled now speeding out of control, she thought about their own safety. She expected that without the musher present and the Musk Oxen no longer in sight, the dogs would stop. But her hope turned to panic as the dogs showed no signs of stopping or slowing down. They continued pulling them across the snow in the wrong direction and away from their parents.

"We need to jump off," she said quickly. "We're getting further away from Mum and Dad every second."

"Are you out of your mind?" Jack protested. "I'm not jumping out of a moving sled!"

"We have to," Poppy said. "We're getting too far away. We'll never find our way back if we keep going."

Jack thought about what she was saying as the dogs slowed down to avoid some rocks up ahead. Poppy saw her opportunity. She hurled herself to the right, grabbing Jack and their bags and dragging them over the edge.

They rolled across the snow several times before stopping, and Poppy could see the dogs running off in the distance.

"You idiot!" Jack shouted.

His reaction was understandable. Poppy hadn't exactly given him much warning.

"If we'd stayed, who knows where we'd end up," she snapped back.

Jack didn't say anything, and Poppy gave them both a minute to calm down while they planned their next move.

"We've travelled in a fairly straight line," she said a few minutes later, pointing at the snow. "If we follow the tracks, we should be able to retrace our steps... we'll need to move quickly, though. If the snow starts falling again, the tracks will be covered."

After walking for a while, Jack pointed to a rock in the distance, "I think we're getting closer, you know. I remember seeing that rock and thinking it looked like a seal."

With each step, their boots sank deep into the snow; their legs were so tired, and after what felt like forever, they saw something in the distance.

"Trees! Do you think that's it?" said Jack.

"I'm not sure, but let's find out," Poppy said, picking up the pace with new energy.

As they got closer, they started calling out for their parents. Over and over, they called out, their voices echoing through the trees, but no one answered.

In need of a break, they sat down on a fallen tree trunk, and Poppy got some water and cereal bars out of her bag.

They sat for a while, trying not to think about the fact that their parents didn't seem to be there.

"Do you think people are looking for us?" Jack asked, looking worried.

"Absolutely," she reassured him, trying to be brave for the both of them.

"Good," he said. "Because I really want to go home now."

"I know me too; it won't be long now."

- CHAPTER THREE -

AN UNEXPECTED ENCOUNTER

Focused on coming up with a plan, Poppy was startled when Jack shook her arm. "Did you hear that?" he asked. She listened carefully, but she couldn't hear anything. Jack sat up straight, "There it is again; I'm telling you, there's something over there, come on!"

Poppy chased after him. "Slow down! We'll lose each other!" she panted.

The trees were thick in this part of the wood, and after being whipped by several branches, Poppy stopped in her tracks as she heard something in the distance.

She could barely make it out, but there was definitely someone talking. "Stop! I hear it too!" she said, almost entirely out of breath.

"I told you," said Jack, running even faster.

As they got closer, the voices were clearer, but the conversation was far from ordinary…

"Well, you've really done it this time, Wren! What are we supposed to do now?" a voice cried. "I have to get back and prepare before the competition, and we still don't have the recipe. I don't know why I let you talk me into this. My recipes were perfectly fine, passed down through generations. Then you got in my head, and now look at us!"

Poppy and Jack looked at each other, feeling confused. What were people doing out here, in the middle of nowhere, arguing about a recipe?

They continued to eavesdrop.

"Giselle! Will you please stop panicking? There's still one more town on the list. I'm sure we'll find it there. I just need to get my bearings again; this blizzard's really knocked us off track," the other voice said in a less-than-confident voice. "I think we're stuck on something. Help me take a look."

Jack edged forward to try and get a look at the people talking, but as he did, a branch snapped underneath him. Poppy held her breath.

"What was that? Did you hear that?" cried Giselle.

"Oh my goodness, will you calm down? It's probably just some snow falling off a branch." Wren said, growing impatient.

"How do you know?" Giselle snorted, "You do know that there are foxes and worse out here that would consider an elf a tasty afternoon snack. Sorry, I'm not in the mood to become someone's lunch!"

Poppy and Jack looked at each other.

"Did she just say 'elf'?" Jack whispered in disbelief.

They kept moving in the direction of the voices, and finally, they reached a clearing.

Poppy's heart skipped a beat. Her eyes couldn't believe what she was seeing.

She looked at Jack to check that he was seeing the same thing because, right in front of them, stood two Christmas elves!

Poppy and Jack's mouths hung open. It was like the elves had stepped right out of the pages of a book - with pointy ears, pointy shoes, rosy cheeks, and striped socks.
"No way!" Jack blurted out, much louder than he had intended, and with that, their presence was finally announced.
"Humans!" shrieked the two elves, their voices filled with panic as they darted behind the cover of a nearby tree.
Poppy couldn't hide her frustration as she shot Jack a furious look.
She approached the tree, attempting to break the ice.
"Sorry if we startled you," she said. "I'm Poppy, and this is my brother Jack. We got lost in the blizzard. We were hoping we might be able to help each other?"
Behind the tree, the two elves remained perfectly still.
"Don't say anything; maybe they'll go away," warned Giselle.
Poppy and Jack waited for a reply, but as the sun moved through the trees, something sparkled in the corner of their eye. They looked around and spotted something. - A snowmobile!
But this was no ordinary snowmobile.
To start with, it was tiny! Poppy wondered if their grandparents, Pomeranian Chester, would even fit on it.
The frame was made from beautifully polished wood, with delicate gold vines winding around the edges.
The handlebars were shaped like antlers and studded with gleaming crystals; that must have been what caught their attention.
"Wow! Is this your snowmobile that's stuck?" Jack called over to the tree. "Can we help you take a look at it?"

Poppy looked at her brother. "What exactly do we know about snowmobiles?" she whispered discreetly out the corner of her mouth.

Behind the tree, the elves remained deathly still.

"This - is - a - disaster," gasped Giselle.

"I know," said Wren seriously, "They'd better not touch my snowmobile."

Giselle looked at him, lost for words. "Are you serious? I wasn't actually thinking about your precious snowmobile, Wren. I was thinking more about the fact that we are outside the North Pole *without* clearance, and now we've been spotted by two humans!"

Wren looked embarrassed at his misunderstanding. "Yes, of course, sorry," he mumbled. "But didn't you hear them? They're lost, too. Maybe they can help us get the snowmobile back on the road? We could get to the last town and be back in the North Pole before anyone notices."

As the elves continued to debate, Poppy and Jack got closer to the snowmobile to investigate.

It was even more impressive up close, with detailed carvings of elves gathered around a Christmas tree and beautiful embroidery on the red velvet seat.

On closer inspection, they saw that the snowmobile's skis were wedged between some rocks.

"I can see where it's stuck." Jack said, "I reckon between us, we can lift it up. If you grab that end and I'll -"

Without another word, an elf came flying out from behind the tree.

"Oh no, you don't! Don't you touch my snowmobile!" he yelled, running towards them with a stick. "Get back before you damage it with your big old human hands."

Poppy found herself wanting to burst into uncontrollable laughter at the sight of this small elf charging towards them. Still, she stopped herself because the elves were making it very obvious that their presence was not welcome here.

Their hopes of a rescue were looking less and less likely. Jack confronted the elf. "Alright, calm down! We didn't touch it, did we? Even if we did, we were only trying to help!"

Poppy stepped in. "We're sorry," she said softly, "We really were only trying to help."

The elf looked at them. He didn't say anything, but her apology seemed to have made things a little better, so Poppy decided to change the subject.

"It's a beautiful snowmobile you have here. I've never seen anything like it," she said.

This compliment worked better than expected. The elf beamed at her with pride.

"She's a beauty, isn't she?" he said. "I did all the carving work myself. Originally, I was going to do scenes from the Workshop, but these designs turned out so much better. It's the first time she's been out in a blizzard. If it weren't for these rocks, I think she would have handled it pretty well. I had the -"

"Ugh," they heard from behind the tree as the second elf finally appeared, looking furious.

"Will you shut up!" she yelled at Wren. "Shut up, shut up, shut up!!" she screeched, hitting him with her scarf on every "shut up."

She glanced over to where Poppy and Jack were standing but avoided making eye contact.

"Sorry, but we need to get going. It was nice to meet you both. We hope you find your way back okay; we must be on our way now." she said, signalling for them to leave. "Oh, and we'd appreciate it if you didn't mention us to anyone," she added.

Poppy and Jack looked at each other, unsure what to do. "You can't send us away!" Jack cried. "Didn't you hear us? We're lost! We'll freeze out here!" he looked desperately at Giselle, who suddenly seemed rather ashamed of herself, realising how selfish she was being.

No one knew what to say next, but eventually, Giselle spoke. "I'm sorry…of course, we will help you," she said. "Although honestly, I don't know how. I mean, even if we can move the snowmobile, you two are far too big to ride it with us."

It was the same thought that had been in the back of Poppy's mind since they'd laid eyes on it. Not to mention, even if they could ride it, they had no idea where they'd be going.

Suddenly, she had an idea. "Where did you guys come from?" Poppy asked. "We heard you talking about some other towns you'd been to. Are they nearby?"

She instantly regretted this question as Giselle's mood shifted from sympathy to annoyance.

"Exactly how long were you snooping on us?" she asked.

"We're so sorry," Poppy said quickly. "We were only being careful. We had no idea who you were. But we overheard you mention other towns and something about a recipe? Maybe you could go back to the town you were in last and let them know we're here so they can send help?"

Giselle laughed. She stopped when she realised Poppy wasn't joking. "My dear, we are elves. We can't simply walk into town and start talking to humans. We shouldn't even be here now talking to you," she said, her eyes filling with tears. "If anyone finds out..." her voice trailed off as she shook her head in her hands.

Poppy rushed to comfort her. "It's okay, we'll think of something else she said, "That was a silly idea; please don't get upset."

She removed her gloves to offer Giselle a pack of tissues from inside her backpack.

"My goodness! You're frozen to the bone," said Wren, observing Poppy's struggle with the zip on her backpack. "Let's start a fire so you two can warm up while we figure this out.

- CHAPTER FOUR -

AN UNUSUAL RESCUE STRATEGY

Poppy and Jack sat, watching the flames dance in the fire as Wren brought over a flask of hot chocolate and some marshmallows for roasting.

It was, without a doubt, the best hot chocolate they had ever tasted. Each sip was better than the last.

Poppy was tired, but she tried to stay alert so she could eavesdrop on the conversation that was taking place a few feet away.

"Have you gone completely bonkers?" Giselle whispered. "Taking them back to the North Pole? It's unheard of!"

Wren, sounding calm and composed, replied, "I can't see any other choice. We can't get help, and we can't leave them here. The portal only goes back to the North Pole. It's the only solution I can think of."

There was more, but Poppy couldn't quite make it out. Eventually, she heard footsteps coming back towards them.

Wren explained their plan. "We have a portal that will take us back to the North Pole," he revealed as Poppy and Jack's jaws dropped to the floor.

"Once we are in the North Pole, we can work on building a new portal to get you back to your parents."

Giselle chimed in to make sure the rules were crystal clear. "Now, if we take you to the North Pole, you must stay completely hidden. Do you understand? It's important. You cannot be seen by anyone. The portal will take us back to my house, and you can stay with me while we create a new one."

"How long would it take?" Poppy asked, thinking of her parents.

"Not long, just a day or two," said Wren.

Poppy was taken aback. "A day or two! Thank you so much for the offer, but we can't stay away for that long; our parents would be worried sick."

Giselle looked puzzled, but Wren understood Poppy's concerns. "We should have explained earlier. I can set the portal to take you back to when you lost your parents. Technically, you won't have been lost at all!"

Jack, who had been sat in stunned silence until then, had a question. "Wait, are you talking about time travel?"

Wren tried to explain, "Sort of. Well, yes, and no." Which left them more confused than ever.

Giselle stepped in to give a more detailed explanation. Time travel is fiction; the concept has been completely exaggerated over the years. The ability to go back hundreds of years and change the course of history is a little bit far-fetched, don't you think? What we are talking about here is a time passage, a tunnel, if you will, between two relatively close periods of time. The use of time tunnels is, for obvious reasons, restricted, but it's possible if you know the right elf," she said, looking at Wren.

Wren was eager to move forward with their rescue plan. "So, what do you think? Are we ready to go?"

Poppy didn't know what to do. This was a once-in-a-lifetime opportunity…maybe even a thousand lifetimes. Visions of elves, candy canes, and beautifully decorated Christmas houses danced in her mind; it was a dream beyond compare. But going to the North Pole meant stepping further away from her parents.

How confident were they that this plan would work? What if Wren couldn't take them back to that exact moment?

She stood there, thinking about their options, but in the end, she came to the same conclusion as Wren and Giselle -this was the only plan they had… It had to work!

"Let's do it," she declared.

Jack agreed, "Alright, we're going to the North Pole!" They looked at each other, barely believing the words that had just come out of Jack's mouth.

Wren walked over to the snowmobile and took out what looked like a floating, glittering circle. They could see a living room inside it.

"Is that your house?" Jack asked Giselle.

Giselle nodded, "That's home. Now, if everyone gathers around the edges of the portal, we'll get going."

Suddenly, Poppy thought of a question, "Wait! I'm confused, sorry. If you had this portal, why were you arguing about being lost earlier? Why didn't you just go home?"

Giselle was clearly annoyed. "Well, this is what happens when you snoop, isn't it. You get only half the story. We needed to go somewhere else to find something important before going home."

Not satisfied with this answer, Poppy continued, "You mentioned a recipe. You were looking for a recipe?" Giselle sighed, growing tired of Poppy's questions, "Yes, if you must know, Mrs Nosey Pants, we were trying to find a recipe for an important competition in the North Pole. But we got stuck, and now we need to get home to help you two ungrateful humans. So, please, for the last time, let's gather around the edges of the portal so we can get moving!"

"Alright, everyone," Wren said, trying to lighten the mood. "We need to lift the portal over our heads and stretch it out so it covers us and the snowmobile. Once we're all in position, I'll shout 'go,' and then you need to drop the portal to the ground, making sure you're on the inside. Make sense?"

Everyone nodded as they began arranging themselves accordingly. Despite some challenges presented by their height difference, they got into formation fairly quickly. "Okay, ready! One, two, three, DROP!" Wren yelled.

Poppy thought she'd feel queasy, like when you got off a roller-coaster, but she felt fine. Everything happened so quickly she didn't have time to feel anything, and now, here they were, in Giselle's living room - in the North Pole!

Poppy quickly looked around the room to make sure everyone was okay. Jack was fine, already gazing around the room in amazement. Meanwhile, Giselle hurriedly checked the curtains, ensuring they were as tightly closed as possible, and Wren tended to the fire.

"I didn't think we'd be able to stand up properly in here, but it's even bigger than our living room back home!" Jack said.

"Oh yes, Santa's orders," said Wren. "Elf homes used to be a lot smaller, but after a few hundred years, Santa was getting such terrible backache from stooping down all the time that now all ceilings in the North Pole have to be at least eight feet tall."

Poppy took off her coat and looked around.

Giselle's house was amazing, like two small front rooms stacked on top of each other, connected by a spinning ladder. The lower part had bookshelves with colourful fairy lights and an enormous collection of snow globes. Higher up in the room, there were fantastic murals and tapestries celebrating the wonders of Christmas. Santa, Mrs Claus, and elves came to life with animations like twinkling lights and gently falling snowflakes. Every detail in the room was a work of art.

Next to the fireplace was a stunning Christmas tree covered in red, green, and gold baubles, with elaborate ribbons draped down the sides.

Poppy couldn't help but think of her mum; she would have loved this.

"My dear, what's wrong! Are you hurt?" asked Wren, concerned.

Poppy wiped away a tear. "Oh no, nothing like that. It's been a very long day, that's all. You have a lovely home, Giselle; thank you so much for sharing it with us. Sorry if I didn't seem grateful before."

Giselle stopped her frantic scurrying and looked at Poppy for the first time with a genuine smile.

"You're welcome, Poppy. It's been a long day. I think what we need is something to eat and a good night's sleep so we can all start fresh tomorrow?"

Poppy couldn't have been happier to hear these words; she was utterly exhausted.

Wren decided this was his cue to leave, so they helped him move his snowmobile into the hallway. At the same time, Giselle fluttered around, making sure they didn't accidentally open the front door and get spotted.

"Where do you live, Wren? Is it nearby?" asked Jack.

"I've got an apartment above the stables," Wren replied. "It's not too far from here."

Giselle made sure that Poppy and Jack were safely returned to the living room with the door closed before opening the front door to see Wren off. Jack waited until she was out of earshot before he spun around.

"Can you believe this place!" he said excitedly.

"We're in the North Pole! This is unbelievable! Did you see the paintings up there moving? That girl kind of looks like you," he said without taking a breath.

Poppy looked up. Actually, he was right. The girl did look a bit like her—pale skin, auburn hair, and thick eyebrows. Still, the girl in the painting was wearing a hideously thick, orange cable-knit jumper that Poppy wouldn't be caught dead in.

Giselle walked back into the room. "Alright, who's hungry? Let's get something to eat," she said, leading them toward a door on the other side of the room.

The kitchen was much more elf-sized. The countertops, stove, and cabinets were all scaled down to the right height, and the spaces on the walls above were filled with garlands of herbs, peppers, and dried fruits.

"Gingerbread pumpkin soup alright for everyone?" Giselle asked. Jack looked concerned, but Poppy, not wanting to be rude or upset Giselle any further today, lied, "Sounds delicious! Can we help with anything?"

"Oh, thank you, there's some bread in the pantry. Jack, if you could set the table, please."

Poppy checked the pantry - inside was full of every kind of baking tool imaginable - cookie cutters, mixing spoons, rolling pins, scales, sprinkles, icing, edible glitter, and more. Poppy had never seen such an enormous collection.

After some searching, she found the bread and closed the door as a concerned Jack appeared next to her.

"Have you seen the size of these bowls?" he whispered, holding one up. "I'm going to need about seven of them!"

"I'm sure there'll be enough," she laughed, "If not, you can have some of mine."

"That's if I even want more! Did you hear what she said? Gingerbread pumpkin!" Poppy told him to stop being rude and sent him away to finish setting the table.

It was quite a squeeze to all sit together, but at least Jack seemed to have gotten over his concerns about the soup as he wolfed down a second and third helping.

Poppy had to admit, when she first heard the words "Gingerbread pumpkin," she'd also been a little concerned, but the soup was delicious - a North Pole staple, according to Giselle.

Thick and velvety, made with roasted pumpkin, ginger, cinnamon, and nutmeg, garnished with a dollop of cream and a generous sprinkle of gingerbread.

They ate in silence, too tired to chat.

As they finished, Giselle thought about the sleeping arrangements. "The beds aren't going to be big enough for you, so we'll have to make up a bed on the floor. Is that okay?" she said apologetically.

They went to the spare room and set up a bed using blankets and pillows, and Giselle also realised she didn't have pyjamas that would fit.

"That's fine; we've got about a hundred layers of clothing. We'll manage." Poppy laughed.

"Okay, do you need anything else?" Giselle asked. "I've put some toothbrushes in the bathroom for you, but if you think of anything else, I'll be right next door…believe it or not, it's my first time hosting humans." She added with a wink as she left the room.

"You know, I think she's starting to warm up to us," smiled Jack as they flopped onto their pillows for a good night's sleep.

- CHAPTER FIVE -

THE NORTH POLE

Soft, golden sun, flickering through the seams of the curtains, woke Poppy the following day. Beside her, Jack was still fast asleep. She was desperate to go and look out the window, but their promise to stay hidden stopped her. A promise she was determined to keep.

The bed they'd made for themselves turned out to be pretty comfortable. Poppy laid her head back down, only to be lured back up by the scent of pancakes wafting in from the kitchen.

"Jack, wake up," she said, prodding him. He stirred briefly before going back to sleep. In the end, a flick of his ear did the trick.

"Is that pancakes?" he said, now wide awake.

"Smells like it," she said.

After briefly debating what they should wear to breakfast, they settled on their thermal leggings, vests, and jumpers before making their way out to the kitchen, where Giselle was hard at work.

"Good morning, how did you sleep? She asked brightly. "I hope I didn't wake you. I was just making a start on breakfast, the most important meal of the day. Have a seat; this batch won't be much longer." Giselle pointed at the table, which had been set with a lace tablecloth and glass bottles holding sprigs of holly.

Poppy couldn't help but notice the four plates of pancakes already sat in the middle. Were they expecting more guests?

Seeing Poppy's confusion, Giselle explained, "I wasn't sure what kind of pancakes humans liked, so I made buttermilk, blueberry, banana, vanilla, and chocolate chip ones. Sit down and enjoy before they get cold."

Poppy and Jack filled their plates with one of each flavour.

"These pancakes are amazing, Giselle. They're the fluffiest pancakes I've ever had in my life." Jack said.

Giselle beamed with pride. "Thank you very much. I'm so pleased you like them," she said, glowing with happiness.

Poppy was determined to keep the positive conversation going. "I noticed you have a lot of baking stuff in the pantry. Do you do a lot of baking?"

Giselle expertly flipped the last batch of pancakes and sat down with them. "Oh yes, baking is in my blood," she explained. "My mother and my grandfather were incredible bakers. They founded The Sugar & Snowflake Bakery, where I work. It's one of the most prestigious bakeries in the North Pole."

Poppy felt terrible for not considering that Giselle might have had other plans today beyond supervising them.

"If you need to be somewhere today, don't worry about us. We know the rules – no going outside or near the windows."

"Thank you, but I'm not working today; I'm preparing for the great North Pole Bake-Off," she said excitedly.

"What's that?" Jack asked with a mouth full of more pancakes.

Giselle seemed genuinely surprised that he hadn't heard of it. "Why, it's only the biggest baking competition in all of the North Pole!" she said. The winner gets the incredible honour of making the cookies and confections for the Snow Ball."

"It sounds wonderful," said Poppy. "If these pancakes are anything to go by, I'm sure you'll win."

After breakfast, they tried to help clean up, but Giselle redirected them to the living room to prevent accidents after Jack experienced several near-collisions with the kitchen shelves.

Poppy decided to take a shower and left Jack admiring the snow globe collection.

She walked down the hall and pushed open the bathroom door, where her hopes of showering immediately crumbled.

The bathtub was no bigger than a large sink, so she settled instead for a quick wash and brushing her teeth. It felt quite nice, after all the chaos and excitement of the past twenty-four hours, to do something as normal as brushing her teeth.

Poppy's days were usually pretty predictable. Like most people, she had a routine. She wasn't obsessive about it, but there was a general plan. Today, she had no idea what would happen, and she couldn't quite work out if she was excited or terrified about that.

Teeth cleaned, Poppy headed back down the hall, where a familiar voice came from the front room.

Wren had arrived.

She could hear him talking to the others. "Santa himself has been using this for years; it's perfectly safe," he said.

As she walked in, Wren, Giselle, and Jack were all gathered around the fireplace. Wren was holding something in his hand that had everyone's attention.

"Poppy, come join us," he said eagerly, passing whatever was in his hand to her.

"This is Santa's Shrinking Potion," he said. "It's the perfect disguise so you and Jack can come and help me with the portal today."

Poppy's uncertainty as she came into the room gave way to excitement. If Wren said they needed a disguise, it must mean they were going outside!

Her excitement, however, was short-lived.

"I'm not sure about this," said Giselle. "Height isn't the only problem. What about their ears?"

"All they need is a change of clothes, boots, and some earmuffs to cover their ears. No one will know the difference." Giselle didn't look convinced.

"Think about it," he continued, "The sooner we can finish this portal, the sooner everything can get back to normal."

This struck a chord with Giselle. She was positively glowing at the thought of returning to normal, precisely as Wren had intended.

"Okay, fine," she said, "Let's try."

Wren measured out several doses of shrinking potion on one side of the room. While Giselle searched for suitable outfits for them on the other. Poppy had to laugh at how quickly Giselle shifted from disliking the plan to finding them the perfect outfits. The thought of returning to normal had really motivated her.

Wren was now heading towards them, holding what looked like a jar of rainbows for each of them.

Poppy raised her glass and clinked it with Jack's.
"Cheers," she said before downing the sweet and slightly
sour liquid. A strange tingling sensation spread
throughout her whole body as the world around her grew
larger and larger. The ceiling was so much further away
now, and she found herself looking Wren directly in the
eyes for the first time, noticing fine lines in his skin that
she hadn't seen before.
Jack was clutching at his vest and trousers, "Hey! Our
clothes have shrunk, too!"
Wren, slightly confused by Jack's statement, replied,
"Well, of course. Santa can't be changing in and out of
clothes all night on the busiest day of the year, can he?"
"Santa uses this to deliver everyone's presents?" Jack
asked, fascinated.
"Of course, how else do you think he would fit down the
chimney?" said Wren. "Well, actually, chimneys are a bit
of a thing of the past now, aren't they? Most of these
modern homes don't have one. The majority of last year's
deliveries were actually made via cat flap."
He started to walk out of the room. "You'll have to keep
taking the potion, or it will wear off, but there's more
over there for when you need it. I gave you a high dose
that will last the day. I'm going to go and find Giselle.
Why don't you two get changed, and then we'll head off."
Poppy burst into laughter as Jack revealed his outfit, but
her amusement was interrupted as she saw Wren and
Giselle returning to the room carrying a full-length
mirror.
"Oh, you both look wonderful," Giselle said, handing
Poppy a beautiful pair of cream earmuffs. "Come, look at
yourselves and tell us what you think."

Jack rushed over, clearly concerned by Poppy's reaction. "It looks like I'm wearing a dress!" he said. "Wait... is it a dress?" he asked, puzzled.

Wren and even Giselle joined in the laughter. "No, boy, it's a tunic. Put the belt on with it, and it will be perfect," Wren assured him, offering him a thick black belt. Jack took it and tried it on but still didn't seem entirely convinced.

"Shall we head out then? There's work to be done." Wren urged, walking towards the hallway.

They followed him outside, where they spotted his amazing snowmobile.

As their eyes adjusted to the daylight, they were amazed by the breath-taking beauty beyond the end of the driveway.

The North Pole stretched out in all directions, covered in pristine, glistening snow that sparkled like a million diamonds under the sun. Between the trees were pockets of colourful houses, their roofs covered with twinkling lights and decorations. Lazy plumes of smoke rose from the chimneys while elves bustled about on cobblestone streets lined with holly bushes and lanterns.

The cheerful laughter of elves filled the air as groups made their way toward a huge frozen lake to enjoy some ice skating. In the centre of the lake stood an extraordinary fountain, complete with a life-size statue of Santa.

Incredible ice sculptures had been carved on the ice, each one lit up in different colours. They took a few steps forward, trying to absorb every detail of this magical place.

As they stood looking out, they could tell that Giselle and Wren were also lost in the moment. Appreciating their wonderful home through fresh eyes.

"It's remarkable, isn't it?" said Wren with pride as he hopped on the snowmobile, patting the seat behind him. Poppy and Jack climbed on as Wren passed them two helmets.

Nobody passing by paid any attention to them - so far, they were blending in pretty well.

"Hold on tight!" Wren warned. And with that, the snowmobile's engine roared to life and began moving forward.

"Good luck! Be careful!" They heard Giselle shout as she waved them goodbye.

- CHAPTER SIX -

SANTA'S STABLES

The snowmobile picked up speed, smoothly gliding over the snow, leaving behind a trail of sparkles that glittered in its path.

It wasn't just because they were smaller now. Everything was so much bigger than Poppy had ever imagined - the buildings, the streets, the statues.

She'd always imagined the North Pole to be a long street leading up to a giant Workshop, but the North Pole was actually quite vast.

There were so many questions swirling in her mind, but she knew Wren couldn't hear them over the loud engine's roar as they sped along.

They were moving away from the houses and into a more wooded area. "Look there!" Wren yelled over the wind, pointing at a massive wooden gate, all lit up, with a sign above that said "Santa's Stables."

Suddenly, it hit Poppy. When Wren had mentioned he lived in an apartment above the stables, she didn't think anything of it. But he meant the stables! The stables where Santa kept his reindeer and, most likely, his legendary sleigh. She was stunned by this incredible surprise.

They carried on down a winding path, illuminated by streetlights shaped like candy canes, and at the end, they reached a large airfield.

In the middle was a long runway lined with colourful lights and red-and-white stripes down the centre.

At the far end stood a hangar with a giant festive wreath above the door. The door was open, and Poppy gasped as she peered inside.

"I can't believe it! Santa's sleigh," she whispered. She desperately wanted to stop and look closer look, but they continued toward the stable buildings behind the airfield.

Wren parked next to a staircase that led to the upper floors. Poppy and Jack hopped off the snowmobile and instantly started firing countless questions at him.

"Okay, okay, slow down," he laughed. "Let's have a cup of tea first, then we can talk." They followed him upstairs and to the right, where Wren opened the door to his apartment.

This time, they were left speechless for an entirely different reason...

Wren's apartment was in total chaos! It reminded Poppy of a mad scientist's laboratory. Tools and random bits of wood and metal were scattered across every surface and walkway. Wren cleared a path to the sofa.

"Sorry about the mess," he said cheerfully. "I don't get many visitors. Usually, we gather in the common rooms downstairs, so this room has become a bit of a workshop for my personal projects."

He wandered over to the other side of the room and picked up something that looked like a water gun. "This nifty little gadget is the Tinsel Twirler Five Hundred!" he declared. "It can decorate up to twenty Christmas trees with tinsel in five hundred seconds or less."

Poppy and Jack shared a smile, noticing that most of Wren's projects were far from finished.

"What do you do in the North Pole, Wren?" Jack asked, looking around the room with curiosity.

"I'm part of team YuleTrek," he replied proudly, pointing to the YuleTrek plaque hanging above the fireplace.

"Right… and what is that, sorry?" said Jack.

"Well, it's like an engineer," Wren explained. "Our focus is route strategy and aerodynamic advancement."

Jack still looked lost.

"In other words, our job is to plan the best route for Santa on Christmas Eve and ensure the sleigh and everything are in tip-top shape." Now Jack was seriously impressed.

They cleared some more items out of the way to make space to sit down while Wren went to the kitchen to make tea. They glanced around at Wren's other projects. The one closest to them was some kind of hoverboard, according to the drawings next to it. This clever device allowed elves to load ornaments into the basket and hover up to decorate the top branches of any tree.

Wren returned shortly after. "So, where were we?" he asked, setting a tray of tea on the table in front of them.

"You were going to tell us what we need to do today," Poppy reminded him, hoping he wasn't overestimating their abilities!

"Ah, yes," he said, picking up some papers he'd knocked over on the way. "We need to go to the ice caves to get more Chrono Quartz for the portal. We've run out at YuleTrek with Christmas Eve coming up, and we won't harvest again until the New Year."

"Caves?" Poppy asked, feeling anxious. "What kind of caves? Are they safe?"

"Perfectly safe, just tricky to navigate alone," Wren reassured her.

Jack then asked Poppy's next question, "What's Chrono Quartz?"

"It's for the portal," Wren explained. "Chrono Quartz gives a portal the ability to move through time; it's only found in the caves near the North Pole." Jack's eyes widened with fascination.

"So, what was the portal we used yesterday?" Jack asked.

"That portal didn't have any Chrono Quartz," Wren said. "That's what we call an A to B portal, allowing us to move quickly from one place to another."

"I wish we had those for getting to school," Jack said.

Wren chuckled, "It's not that simple, I'm afraid. While useful in the right situations, both portals are hard to build and don't last more than a week before becoming unstable. They're perfect for Christmas Eve, though, to help Santa travel the world in one night."

"How far are the caves?" Poppy asked.

"Not too far," Wren said. "But we'll need to walk for the last bit because the entrance is in an ice boulder field."

When Wren said he needed their help today, Poppy had imagined herself holding the odd screwdriver or making cups of tea. This was turning into a full-scale expedition! "Don't let your tea get cold," Wren said, handing them each a cup.

As they sipped their tea, Wren shared more details about the work of YuleTrek. Poppy was amazed by how complex their operation was.

They had to consider so many things: weather conditions, new housing developments, time zones, reindeer energy levels, and how gifts were loaded on the sleigh. Every single detail was precisely planned down to the last moment to ensure that everyone got their gifts on time.

"Alright, let's get to work," Wren finally announced after Poppy and Jack had fired countless questions at him. "This portal won't build itself."

They followed Wren out of the front door, and Jack made a beeline for the stairs down to the snowmobile.

"This way, Jack. We're not using the snowmobile for this," said Wren.

Slightly confused about how they would get to the caves, Poppy and Jack followed Wren down the other stairs in the opposite direction and crossed a courtyard.

Wren swung open the door, and they were met by the most beautiful sight of Santa's famous reindeer.

"Meet the team," Wren said cheerily, leading them inside.

The stable was warm and cosy. Each reindeer had a stall with straw, soft blankets, and a window overlooking the North Pole. There was a food preparation area with carrots, apples, and reindeer feed, and on the walls hung pictures and portraits of the reindeer. Lanterns and festive decorations dangled from the honey-brown beams. In the corner, the reindeer had their very own Christmas tree.

"Are they listening to the radio?" Jack asked, amused.

"Oh yes, they love it," replied Wren.

Poppy walked along the stalls, reading the silver nameplates on each one: "Dasher, Dancer, Prancer, Vixen, Comet, Cupid, Donner, Blitzen, and..."

"It's Rudolph!" Jack exclaimed with excitement. "Poppy, come see!"

She rushed over, and there stood Rudolph, his soft brown fur and friendly eyes above his legendary bright red nose. He curiously wandered over to them, "He wants to say hello," said Wren. "Here, give him a carrot; they're his favourite, especially with a bit of icing sugar! He's got a bit of a sweet tooth, has our Rudolph."

Jack offered the carrot, and Rudolph eagerly licked off the icing sugar before taking a bite. "Good boy," said Wren, gently patting Rudolph's neck.

Wren then directed their attention to another stall. "Looks like someone's feeling left out," he said with a smile. Poppy saw Blitzen looking at them from a neighbouring stall. "Her favourite is apples," Wren said affectionately. "Fetch one, would you, Poppy?"

Blitzen's fur was more grey than brown. She had smaller antlers and a golden gleam in her eyes.

Poppy felt a connection with her as if they were old friends. She offered the apple in her hand, and Blitzen devoured it while nuzzling Poppy's hand.

"Shall we prepare a sleigh?" Wren suggested, taking Jack by surprise.

"Is this how we're getting to the caves?" Jack asked, bewildered.

"Yes, I need to take these guys out for their exercise anyway, so we might as well get everything done at once," Wren explained as he walked towards a noticeboard on the wall.

"Now let's see... Dasher and Dancer came out with me this morning, but Rudolph and Blitzen haven't had their turn yet. Let's take them since you've already been introduced - Prancer, my boy!" he shouted down to the other end of the stable where Prancer had popped his head out of his stall.

Poppy loved watching the deep connection Wren had with the reindeer.

"It looks like we have ourselves a volunteer," he said.

"Don't we need all the reindeer for the sleigh?" Jack inquired. "That sleigh was huge!"

"Oh, we won't be using Santa's sleigh; that's reserved for him alone," Wren said. "We'll be taking one of the training sleighs."

"Training sleighs?" Poppy asked.

"Yup," said Wren. "Reindeer are herd animals, you see, they have complex social structures. It's good for them to go out in smaller groups to spend quality time together. The reindeer that chooses to lead the sleigh can change based on their mood and the feelings of the group."

Poppy was fascinated by this explanation, and they began helping Wren prepare everything for the journey.

The training sleigh, though far less elaborate than Santa's, was still beautifully crafted. Then came the part Poppy was most curious about: the reindeer had to choose a leader. They laid the reins on the floor and patiently watched as the reindeer made their choices.

Whoever selected the front spot would lead the journey. Today, Prancer would be taking the lead, with Blitzen and Rudolph following.

"That's amazing," Poppy said. "I always thought Rudolph was at the front."

Wren nodded in agreement, "Most people do because of all the songs on the radio. But if you listen carefully, it's a question: "Rudolph, won't you guide my sleigh tonight?" Santa is asking him if he will lead the way."

As they embarked on their journey, Poppy and Jack couldn't wait for the reindeer to fly, but Wren said they needed to burn off some energy on land first.

About halfway to the caves, he surprised them by guiding the reindeer up into the sky, providing them with a breath-taking view of the North Pole below.

They sped along, enjoying every second of this magical ride. "Look at the Ferris Wheel over there," Jack said, pointing to the ground below. "Ah, yes, that's the MerryFest carnival," Wren explained.

"A carnival!" Poppy and Jack exclaimed, their voices filled with amazement.

Wren looked puzzled, "Didn't Giselle tell you about it? She said she did?"

Poppy exchanged a confused look with Jack, unsure what Wren was talking about. "She mentioned a big bake-off competition. Is that what you mean?" she asked.

Wren burst out laughing, which confused Poppy even more.

"That sounds like Giselle," he chuckled. "Completely obsessed with baking, that elf. I can't believe she didn't tell you about everything else. Actually, the bake-off is just one part of MerryFest," he explained. "It's a huge festival across the North Pole leading to Christmas. It's Santa's way of saying thank you for all the hard work over the year."

Poppy and Jack's eyes sparkled with curiosity.

"What other things happen at MerryFest?" Poppy asked, eager for more details.

"Well, there's the carnival you can see down there, and there's the Holly and Ice Market, where the bake-off takes place tomorrow. There's a firework ceremony outside Santa's cottage with a performance from my favourites, The Twinkle Tones. But the peak of it all is the Snow Ball," said Wren.

"Giselle did say something about a Snow Ball, actually," Jack said. "She said that the bake-off winner gets to create the cookies and confections."

Wren nodded, "Yes, that's right. The Snow Ball is a cherished tradition here in the North Pole. It's a night where everyone dresses in their finest attire to celebrate the Christmas traditions passed down through generations. It's a very special event hosted by Santa and Mrs Claus."

Poppy and Jack were entirely captivated by Wren's descriptions of these enchanting celebrations. They bombarded him with questions for the rest of the journey until they reached the edges of the ice fields.

CHAPTER SEVEN

CHRONO QUARTZ

As they got down from the sleigh, Wren handed them each a rubber band with spikes on.
"These will stop you slipping on the ice," he said.
They left the reindeer munching on some hay and headed into the ice field.
Wren expertly guided them through the frozen labyrinth with boulders of ice as big as buses. Eventually, they saw the entrance to a cave and hanging on the wall were several sleds. "Grab a sled", Wren instructed. "It's the fastest way to get to the heart of the cave."
"And what's the fastest way to get out of them?" Poppy joked, thinking about the epic walk back to the surface afterwards.
"Don't worry, I've got that covered." laughed Wren.
"Now follow my lead; when I lean left or right, you do the same until we get to the bottom."
Feeling a mixture of excitement and nerves, they picked a sled and kicked off into the icy depths. The freezing wind brushed past their cheeks, and their excited screams bounced around the walls before disappearing somewhere deep in the cave. They shook themselves off at the bottom and marvelled at the incredible crystal blue ceiling that sparkled above them, courtesy of the ice fields above.

They left the sleds there and continued further into the cave, following Wren, who was using a trail of water droplets along the walls to guide them.

Soon, they arrived at a small hole in the cave floor, and it was clear that Wren wanted to go down it.

"No way!" Poppy said immediately. Even if it meant never going home, there was no chance whatsoever she was going down there.

Wren chuckled, "You don't need to go down. I just need some help with the harness."

Poppy breathed a massive sigh of relief as Wren took out several items from his backpack, including a harness and ropes.

They secured the rope to an anchor frozen solid in the cave wall and slowly lowered Wren down.

About halfway, he told them to hold steady.

With Wren suspended in mid-air, they soon heard the echoing thud of crystals dropping on the cavern floor and exchanged concerned glances. Surely, Wren wouldn't allow these precious items to fall and shatter on the ground?

"That should do it!" Wren shouted, tugging at the rope. "Now, lower me to the bottom, and I'll send the Chrono Quartz up."

Miraculously, all the crystals were still intact as Poppy and Jack pulled them out, sparkling like white diamonds. They set them aside and hoisted Wren back up.

As he emerged, Poppy saw that he was soaking wet. "What happened to you?" she asked.

Wren laughed, "Nothing to worry about; I got caught in the waterfall, that's all."

Poppy was taken aback, "A waterfall in that hole?" she said, feeling increasingly delighted that she hadn't had to go down there.

Wren nodded, "Yes, just a small one; it's the perfect environment for Chrono Quartz."

He shook his head, dislodging tiny icicles from the tips of his hair.

"You're frozen, what can we do?" Poppy asked.

"If you could grab my spare coat from the backpack and the thermos, I'd love a cup of hot chocolate, please," he replied with a grateful smile.

While Wren sipped his hot chocolate and removed the remaining icicles from his hair, Poppy and Jack gathered the Chrono Quartz into his backpack.

The whole time they'd been in the caves, Poppy had an unshakable feeling that they were being watched – like someone or something was keeping an eye on them. But, every time she looked around, there was nothing around. Just as she was about to dismiss these thoughts for the final time, out of nowhere, from behind a huge rock close by, a brilliant, dazzling light shone against the cave wall.

"What was that?" she said, her heart racing as Wren and Jack looked over, also startled by the light.

Seconds later, another flash caught their eye.

"There's definitely something there!" said Jack worriedly.

Wren didn't say anything; he looked utterly flabbergasted. "It can't be," he said. "There's just no way!" He inched forward for a better view as Poppy's voice trembled with fear, "What's going on?" she asked.

Wren still didn't say anything, trying to get a closer view, but after a third flash, he finally spoke. "I think it's an Aurora Wolf," he said, a look of total astonishment on his face.

Poppy was terrified. If he just said "wolf," shouldn't they be running?

"Aurora Wolf? I thought you said these caves were safe?" Jack said, sounding just as concerned as Poppy.

Wren definitely seemed more amazed than terrified, which reassured Poppy a little.

"Legends speak of the Aurora Wolves as the original guardians of the North Pole," Wren explained, "But they're believed to be extinct; no one I know of has ever seen one, even Santa. There's just no way -"

"Maybe they came back because they know we are imposters," said Jack, attempting to hide his discomfort with humour.

Poppy knew Jack was joking, but she couldn't help wondering if he might actually be onto something, and this might be a real possibility.

To her discomfort, it looked like Wren was considering the same. "I really don't know," he said. "But it would certainly explain the interest in us."

Concern crossed all of their faces.

"What should we do?" asked Jack worriedly.

Wren was deep in thought, "I'm trying to remember a song they taught us at school about them. It was something like, "If your heart holds no harm, they'll stand by your side, but I can't remember the rest."

He kept thinking and finally came to a conclusion. "We should make a gesture to show we mean no harm," he said. "Hand me my backpack. I've got some food in there for the reindeer."

They rolled some apples out toward the rocks and waited. Nothing happened at first, but a few minutes later, not one but three wolves revealed themselves: a mother and two cubs!

Poppy was both mesmerized and petrified. Their fur looked like it had been woven from the very essence of the northern lights. A shimmering tapestry of green, violet, pink, and blue.

The cubs began nibbling on the apples, but the mother's eyes were fixed on them. Warily assessing their intentions.

Wren tried to reassure them. "Stay still and don't break eye contact; she'll see that we mean no harm to them or the North Pole."

Although not entirely convinced (especially since this was also Wren's first encounter with an Aurora Wolf), they continued to wait.

Eventually, she lifted her long, bushy tail into the air. She swayed it gracefully from side to side, like a wave of acceptance and bowed her head to each of them as a mark of respect. At last, she turned her back on them to join the cubs in the feast of apples.

They stood observing them, captivated by the moment; they were the most beautiful creatures Poppy had ever seen, but soon, all three disappeared back into the depths of the cave.

Wren was gobsmacked. "In all my life, I never dreamed I would meet an Aurora Wolf," he said. "And to witness not one, but three! It's unbelievable!"

On the way back to the sleds, Jack and Wren were deep in conversation about the Aurora Wolves, but Poppy couldn't quite bring herself to share their excitement. She kept thinking about what Wren said.

If the Aurora Wolves really were the ancient guardians of the North Pole and they were here now, wasn't this a sign that they were needed for something?

A sign that something bad may be coming?

They returned to the sleds, where Poppy put her concerns aside and was curious to know what Wren's solution was for getting them back to the surface. He opened a bag they'd left with the sleds earlier on and presented them with something.

"The 'Sled Propeller,'" he announced proudly.

He attached it to the front of his own sled, and then, using a system of ropes, he linked Poppy and Jack's sleds behind his, creating an impromptu sled train.

"Hold on tight," he said as he turned it on, and with a nerve-wracking burst of speed, they were propelled back toward the surface.

Back at the sleigh, they readied the reins, and this time, Blitzen stepped forward to lead them back.

After unpacking the sleigh back at the stables, Wren took the remaining reindeer out to the paddocks for some exercise, leaving Poppy and Jack with the task of placing the Chrono Quartz in a shallow bath back at his apartment.

Jack was talking about MerryFest for the thousandth time, his mop of unruly brown hair practically bouncing off his head with excitement as he perched on the edge of the bath, doing very little to help Poppy with the Chrono Quartz.

"We have to go," he said. "We just have to! What if we just ask Wren and Giselle if there is any chance -?"

Poppy looked at him. She didn't even need to say anything.

"Okay, maybe we just ask Wren," he said, grinning as they walked back towards the front door. "But come on, wouldn't it be amazing?"

Poppy was also desperate to see MerryFest; she nodded in agreement as she opened the front door. "We can ask, but I think we both know the answer to -"

"Oh, hello!" said an elf just about to knock. "That was good timing! Is Wren home?"

Poppy and Jack froze.

"Sorry, I didn't mean to startle you," they continued. "I was just looking for Wren. Is he in?"

Poppy and Jack shook their heads, not knowing what to say.

The elf looked troubled. "Okay, any idea when he might be back?" Poppy and Jack shook their heads for a second time.

The elf looked distracted and started to walk away, but he suddenly turned back and asked them again. "You really have no idea at all? Sorry, but it's quite urgent that I speak with him,"

Panic welled in Poppy's chest. This was it! They'd only been alone in the North Pole for ten minutes, and they'd been discovered! How did he find out?

Maybe he lived near Giselle and saw them arrive? But they'd been so careful, that couldn't be it.

Suddenly, Poppy had another thought. Had the pressure gotten too much for Giselle? Had she turned them in? Would she do that?

Her mind racing, the elf finally put Poppy out of her misery as he explained that the Ferris Wheel at the carnival had broken down and they needed Wren's help to fix it before the big fireworks display tonight.

Jack's face lit up, sensing his opportunity, and before Poppy could stop him, he opened his mouth.

"You know what! Now that I think of it, Wren did say something about going to see the reindeer. We'll take you," he said, purposely not looking at Poppy.

The elf looked so relieved. "Oh, brilliant! Thank you so much! My name is Mohan, by the way," he said, extending his hand to shake theirs.

"Poppy," Poppy said nervously, wondering if she should have given a fake name.

"Jack," said Jack, shaking Mohan's hand enthusiastically.

"I've not seen you two around here before; how do you know Wren?" Mohan asked, making polite conversation.

"Family friend," said Jack, changing the subject quickly to ask more about the broken Ferris Wheel.

They went with Mohan down to the stables, where Wren was busy chopping carrots. He nearly chopped his finger off when he saw Poppy and Jack with Mohan! He came running over, "Mohan, good to see you," he said nervously, obviously surprised. "What are you doing back? I thought everyone was at the carnival all day?"

Mohan explained the situation with the Ferris Wheel and asked Wren if he would come and take a look.

Wren looked conflicted. He was well aware that Giselle would never approve of this, but he also couldn't ignore the hopeful expressions on Poppy and Jack's faces.

Sensing Wren's doubts, Mohan attempted to lighten the mood. "It's quite something, isn't it?" he said. "We can get Santa around the world in one night, but this Ferris Wheel's got us stumped! We should do away with it and get one of those virtual reality machines, but Mrs. Claus would never forgive us for that."

In the meantime, Wren seemed to have made up his mind.

"We'll head over on the snowmobile and meet you at the Carnival entrance," he said to Mohan, who looked thrilled.

Poppy and Jack couldn't believe it!

They were going to MerryFest!

- CHAPTER EIGHT -

MERRYFEST

After thanking Wren a million times, they set off for
MerryFest on the snowmobile.

As they cruised along, they passed under a huge bridge that
had been completely transformed into a dazzling MerryFest
sign that lit up the sky. In the moments after, they found
themselves wishing for eyes in the back of their heads to
fully absorb all the incredible things surrounding them.

Everywhere they looked, there were banners and billboards
promoting roller coasters, whimsical carnival games, and an
endless selection of Christmas-themed treats.

In the distance, peering over the rooftops, they caught their
first glimpse of the Ferris Wheel. Instead of the traditional
Ferris Wheel carts that they were used to at home, this one
took you around on tiny sleighs.

Near it, they could also see the tip of a towering Christmas
crowned with an impressive star and countless twinkling
lights that cast a warm glow over the town.

As they drew closer to the town centre, it was a scene of
pure Christmas delight. Both young and old, wrapped up in
their cosiest winter clothes. Scarves in a kaleidoscope of
different colours and woolly hats of all shapes and sizes.
Puffy winter coats made everyone look like colourful,
walking snowballs, and the streets were lined with garlands
and sparkling lights, enticing them towards the carnival.

They parked up and headed for the main square.

Laughter and the gentle voices of carol singers danced in the crisp air. Food carts offered a mouth-watering selection of traditional festive treats like roasted chestnuts, gingerbread, and mince pies, alongside more unusual offerings like Candy Cane Sushi Rolls and Tacos with Peppermint Guacamole.

"Do you guys want to go and explore?" said Wren. "I'll probably need about an hour, and I'll meet you back at The Nutcracker," he pointed down the street. "You can't miss it; it's just down there on the right."
Poppy and Jack were caught entirely off guard by this unexpected freedom to explore alone. Before they could confirm they'd heard him correctly, Wren had spotted Mohan and was off, engrossed in a conversation about the Ferris Wheel.
They moved into the quieter side streets, away from the bustling carnival crowds, while they got their bearings. All the shops were closed for the carnival, but the window displays alone were breath-taking.
Toy Shops filled with all kinds of toys, ranging from timeless wooden classics to cutting-edge technology. Across the way, decoration shops gleamed with stunning displays of wreaths, garlands, and ornaments.
One particular shop, "Frosty's Mitten and Boot Emporium," was piled high with delicately embroidered mittens and matching boots picturing beautifully stitched Christmas scenes. Poppy was fascinated as she stood, thinking about the incredible artistry and dedication that must have gone into crafting a single pair of these stunning items.
Jack was keen to share a discovery of his own and waved Poppy over to a nearby sweet shop. The window was filled with every flavour of candy cane imaginable.

He excitedly read off the labels one by one, changing his mind every second about which one he wanted to try first. There were fashionable boutiques like Arctic Outfitters, which had everything your average elf might need for an adventure through the North Pole. Art galleries showcased stunning work from budding elf artists who were inspired by the festivities that defined their world.

They stood looking in the window of a music store, enjoying the names of the bands like "Frost Fighters" and "The Rolling Snowflakes." Poppy also spotted some albums from the Twinkle Tones on display.

Their most enchanting discovery yet was the Snow Globe Emporium. A spellbinding shop overflowing with snow globes that each housed a miniature realm of winter magic within.

"These are just like the ones at Giselle's house," said Jack excitedly.

Stopping briefly, they soon heard what sounded like rollercoaster screams from up ahead.

Without a word, they ran up the street to check it out.

The loudest screams came from a ride called "Santa's Runaway Sleigh." But deciding that they'd had enough of runaway vehicles for one week, they opted for the "Snowflake Spin" instead. It was a rollercoaster with seats shaped like giant snowflakes that you could move and spin as you went around the track.

Jack convinced Poppy to go on the next ride called "Yeti's Revenge", which took you up the side of a steep mountain before plunging you into the darkness of the Yeti's lair, where he tried to snatch riders from their carts that were being spun around.

Poppy sat the next one out and let Jack go alone. "Snowball Fling," where you sat in giant snowballs flung high into the air.

Poppy had done a similar ride in Spain with Mrs Brown a couple of years ago and vowed never to do it again.

Needing a break from thrill rides, they decided to try a more leisurely ride called "Stocking Swirl," where you stood inside your own stocking that climbed a thirty-foot pole and slowly spun you around at the top, giving an incredible view of the carnival below.

Of course, a visit to the carnival would only be complete with a turn on the Carousel, a dazzling tribute to arctic animals featuring Polar Bears, Arctic foxes, Penguins, Seals, Reindeer, and Huskies.

They explored the carnival games like "Hook a Snowman," "Reindeer Ring Toss," "Icicle Darts," and "Penguin Bowling." Poppy's favourite game, and one that she was surprisingly good at, was called Snowball Santa, where you used slingshots to launch snowballs at stacked Santa targets. Eventually, the smell of all the fantastic food surrounding them became too hard to ignore, and they stopped at a nearby cart to check out the menu.

*** MERRYFEST SPECIALS ***

Blizzard Burger
A double burger with lettuce, candy cane bacon and caramelized onion icicles

Festive Frankfurter
Soft fluffy bun with grilled sausage and a cranberry drizzle

Polar Pizza
Thin crust pizza with North Pole cream, infused with hints of garlic and thyme and snow-capped mozzarella.

North Star Nachos
Blue corn tortilla chips topped with salsa and red and green jalapeño slices with a sprinkle of edible gold stars

A very annoying elf stood in line behind them, unable to make up his mind what he wanted, "I do like the sound of the frankfurter, but I think I'd like it on top of the Nachos with some of the candy cane bacon… Hmm I don't know. Maybe I'll just get all of it! It's free isn't it, who cares." he laughed, in an obnoxious manner.

Poppy couldn't help but hope they sent him away with nothing for being so ungrateful.

They were starving now and opted for a Festive Frankfurter each.

As they strolled along enjoying their food, they noticed a group of elves surrounding a large statue. Feeling curious, they went over to see what all the fuss was about. There was nothing particularly distinctive about the status that they could tell - it was just a statue of an elf. Were there any famous elves?

Poppy racked her brains for something she might have heard growing up, but nothing came to mind. Jack spotted a small plaque sticking out from the ground next to it.

"Barnaby Shadowthorn"
Elder of the Elf Council and founder of the Workshop.
May the spirit of giving forever live on in his name.

Behind them, an elf's voice rang out. "Puh! What a load of nonsense! It makes me so angry every time I lay eyes on it! 'May the spirit of giving live on in his name,' he'd be rolling in his grave if he could see the state of things today."

Poppy and Jack were totally stunned by this outburst. The other elves around them ushered their children away and back towards the carnival. The elf who had made this bizarre statement had a friend with her who was smirking in the background, spurring her on even more.

"Everyone at this festival is acting like it's the greatest thing on earth. It's just a smokescreen to distract us from the reality that the mighty Santa Claus single-handedly destroyed Christmas... Our Christmas," she added with a tone of bitterness. As the elf continued her passionate outburst, more elves walking by rolled their eyes, clearly not paying too much attention to her ideas.

"You," she said, pointing at Jack, who looked startled. `What do you think about it all? Do you buy any of this MerryFest nonsense?"

Jack was totally caught off guard and had no idea what to say. Poppy felt fiercely protective of her brother and refused to remain silent; how dare she talk to him like that. "We're huge fans of Santa, thank you very much; he has our full support," she declared firmly, placing a reassuring hand on Jack's shoulder and steering him away from this unpleasant interaction.

As they walked off, she could hear the elf muttering away to her friend, "Typical; what are they teaching them in schools these days? This whole town has gone mad." Poppy rose above it and kept walking, recalling her father's words: "You can't reason with madness."

They stopped a little further on.

"What was that all about?" Jack said, still a little shaken by the encounter. "Absolutely no idea," Poppy said truthfully. "I suppose every town has its share of wildcards, even the North Pole, apparently!"

They both laughed, deciding to move past the unpleasant interaction and not allow it to ruin what had otherwise been a magical afternoon.

"Shall we try and find this Nutcracker place then and wait for Wren?" Poppy suggested. "Yeah, good idea," Jack said. They retraced their steps back to the entrance and followed the road down to the right as Wren had instructed.

He wasn't joking when he said The Nutcracker would be hard to miss! Styled like an enormous Swiss chalet but grander than any they had ever seen, it stretched proudly to about eight stories.

Stunning floral arrangements hung from each balcony, bathed in the warm glow of classic white lights that twinkled from the wooden panels on each floor.

The Nutcracker sign hung proudly above the doors, swaying in the light breeze.

"Is it a pub?" Jack asked, a hint of uncertainty in his voice.

"Looks like it," Poppy replied, "Do you think we'll be allowed in?"

"He wouldn't have said to meet him there otherwise, would he?" said Jack. "Let's go see."

- CHAPTER NINE -

BARNABY SHADOWTHORN

Pushing open the grand doors to The Nutcracker, they were met with an eruption of noise. Laughter and cheerful chatter swirled through the air as they wondered how they would ever find Wren in this crowd.

They moved forward, weaving in and out of the busy tables and eventually spotted him at a table in the corner with a glass of eggnog.

His face lit up as he saw them, and he waved them over. "Oh good, I was beginning to think you might not find me in here. Busy, isn't it? Everyone getting ready for the fireworks," he said as they took their coats off and sat down.

"How did you get on with the Ferris Wheel?" asked Jack.

"Oh, it was nothing," Wren said modestly. "All back up and running now. What about you two? Did you enjoy the carnival?"

Jack launched into a full rundown of every shop, game, and ride they had seen, his excitement overflowing with every word.

"Sounds like you had a great time," Wren said fondly. "And what about you, Poppy? Did you enjoy it as well?

"It was perfect," she said. "So much fun... well, until the end anyway when we ran into this dreadful elf," she added.

"Dreadful?" Wren asked, concerned. "Dreadful, how? No one suspected anything, did they?" he said, cautiously lowering his voice to make sure no one could hear them. "Oh no, nothing like that," she said as Wren relaxed. "She was raving on about how Santa ruined Christmas and some other elf, Barnaby, I think his name was, would be unhappy if he could see how things were today." Wren rolled his eyes, a faint smirk on his lips. "Ah, "The Opposers" were out in force, were they? Can't just let everyone enjoy MerryFest without spewing their negativity everywhere. Don't pay any attention to them; no one else does," he said, his voice returning to a normal volume as he took another sip of eggnog. "The good news is that they are few and far between. Most elves in the North Pole are incredibly friendly. Still, occasionally, you get a few bad apples who try to spoil it for everyone else."

Poppy felt reassured by the words from Wren, but she still didn't quite understand what this elf's issue was in the first place.

"What are they actually upset about, though? The - what did you call them? The Opposers?" she asked.

Wren, sensing that Poppy was not going to let this go, made a suggestion. "Let me go and fetch you guys a drink, and then I'll explain. They do the best milkshakes here; you have to try one."

Wren headed off to the bar. They suspected he'd be gone a while as this place was getting more packed by the second. Still, they didn't mind at all as it gave them a perfect opportunity to sit and observe the fascinating comings and goings of The Nutcracker.

There was a very loud table to their left, watching a game of Ice Hockey on the TV.

"I'm telling you, if they don't make Brody Crosby captain next year, they're fools. Everyone thinks he is too young, but look at how he plays. His speed and puck control are extraordinary; there's no one else like him."

Across from him, a female elf nodded in agreement.

"He is definitely the most exciting player in a long time. The power in his shots is unmatched – he's actually a pretty good goalie as well, but you can't beat Charlie O'Connor for goalkeepers."

They watched as regulars chatted to the servers, clearing tables and working hard to accommodate all the elves piling in from outside on this special night. Wren must have been one of those regulars as he was already walking back to the table. A look of achievement on his face at beating the crowds and carrying two delicious-looking milkshakes.

"Enjoy," he announced as he placed them down on the table in front of them.

The milkshakes really lived up to Wren's glowing recommendation. As they savoured their first sips, Wren saw they were eagerly waiting to hear his story. Settling back in his seat, he smiled.

"So, you want to hear about the origins of Christmas? Let me tell you how it was told to me as a young boy." Poppy and Jack leaned forward as he began.

"Long ago, in a land far beyond the North Star, lay a hidden village nestled deep within the snowy landscape.
This was no ordinary village; it was home to a unique group of beings known as the North Pole Elves.

The elves cherished kindness, community, and love, which they honoured above all else by exchanging beautiful, handcrafted gifts with one another in a celebration known as Christmas.

Within the village lived a council of wise elves who protected their cherished traditions, ensuring that the spirit of Christmas thrived within their hearts.

One cold morning, a lost explorer named Nicholas stumbled upon the village, exhausted and in need of shelter, accompanied by his faithful reindeer.

The elves had never met a human before. But they recognised the goodness in Nicholas's heart and the elders allowed him to stay with them for a while, where he learned about their unique culture and formed deep friendships with the elves.

Nicholas's encounter with the elves left an impression on him. He was so deeply moved by everything he had seen that he shared his desire to bring these traditions back to the rest of the world.

Nicholas believed that Christmas could unite people and bring a shared moment of peace to the many people he had met on his travels.

The elf elders, with their ancient magic, crafted three extraordinary gifts for Nicholas, known as the "Enchanted Trinity," to help fulfil this vision.

The "Stocking of Giving," a magical sack that could house an endless supply of gifts. The "Rocking Horse of Flight," a magnificent wooden horse that would grant the power of flight to his reindeer, and finally, the "Mallet of Merriment," a tool that would give the elves of the North Pole the ability to support him in his mission of creating wondrous gifts for families everywhere.

Nicholas returned to the world as "Saint Nicholas" and later became more commonly known as "Santa Claus." Armed with these magical gifts from the elf elders, he set off on a journey to spread love, kindness, and the joy of giving to children all over the world.

Years later, after sharing the message of Christmas with every corner of the globe, he returned to the North Pole with his wife to live among the elves, where his heart truly belonged.

The elders used the last of their magic to conceal the North Pole so they could carry out their work, protected from the outside world.

And every Christmas Eve, Santa Claus leaves the North Pole in his sleigh to visit families around the world and leave the beautiful gifts created by the elves under their Christmas trees to be discovered on Christmas morning.

Reminding everyone of the spirit of Christmas - a time for love, sharing, and the magic of giving.

And that's how Christmas, a tradition born in the heart of the North Pole, became a worldwide celebration, bringing people together just as the elves and Nicholas had hoped for all those years ago."

As Wren finished, Poppy was overcome with emotion, tears welled in her eyes. She had never appreciated Christmas more. How could that elf have been so hateful?

Wren handed Poppy a tissue, but Jack was still curious. "So where does Barnaby Shadowthorn fit into all of this?" he asked.

"Barnaby was one of the original Elders. A devoted and generous elf - He is the one that gave Christmas its name and built the original Workshop for the elves to make their gifts for one another."

For the next part, he lowered his voice and leaned in so they couldn't be overheard. "The Opposers say that Barnaby disagreed with Nicholas's plan. They say that Barnaby wanted to keep Christmas just for the North Pole, but he was outvoted and overruled by the rest of the council."

Poppy and Jack looked shocked.

"What happened to him?" asked Poppy.

"Over the years, there have been many different versions - none of them true, of course," he added defensively. "Most say he died, bitter and alone in the outer borders of the North Pole, but as I said, it's all absolute nonsense. Barnaby and Santa were the greatest of friends."

Wren was full of emotion towards the end of his explanation; it obviously meant a great deal to him.

"Together, they passed the magic of Christmas onto the world, and that's a legacy to be proud of, I'd say!"

Poppy raised her milkshake in the air and proposed a toast. "To Barnaby," she said.

Wren looked touched by this gesture.

"To Barnaby," they said, clinking their glasses with hers.

The Nutcracker was clearing out a bit now.

"Oh, by the way, I called Giselle while I was getting your milkshakes. She's going to join us for the fireworks," he said, smiling.

"I left out the part about not making any progress on the portal today; I'd appreciate it if we could keep that part between us," he said with a wink. "There'll be plenty of time to catch up tomorrow."

He looked over at the door, "Actually, that might be her now; let me go check."

- CHAPTER TEN –

FIREWORKS

Poppy and Jack went to greet Giselle, who was wearing a bright red jumper covered in sparkling sequin fireworks over her dress.

She was pleased to see them, but Poppy could tell she was uneasy about being with them in public. She couldn't help but wonder how persuasive Wren had been in convincing her to come along.

With their group assembled, they followed the crowds down to Santa's cottage for the display.

Santa's cottage! Poppy couldn't believe it. Did this mean they would be seeing Santa himself? The thought overwhelmed her with excitement.

The crowd outside the cottage was enormous! Poppy couldn't believe how many elves lived in the North Pole. It was so different from the crowds she was used to at home; here, everyone was remarkably polite and orderly.

They hadn't long to wait before the Twinkle Tones graced the stage in a fifteen-member strong choir. Wren and Giselle swayed along and knew all the lyrics by heart. Poppy didn't recognise the songs, but even so, she was enchanted by the beauty of their voices. Even Jack looked like he was enjoying it.

Santa's cottage was a Christmas dream come true.

The front door was a masterpiece, crafted from solid wood and painted bright red, featuring numerous stained glass windows. Each window told a tale of Santa's Workshop, and in the centre of the door, a brass knocker shone, reflecting the lights surrounding the cottage.

In the garden, a family of snowmen had been dressed for the occasion in colourful top hats and scarves.

The crowd cheered as they bid farewell to the Twinkle Tones and welcomed the evening's host to the stage. Poppy was captivated by his unique appearance - a bit crow-like, with glossy black hair, a pointed nose, and small, beady eyes that stood in stark contrast to his rosy cheeks.

"Good evening, North Pole! Is everyone having a jolly time at MerryFest?" he bellowed into the crowd, sparking even louder cheers and applause.

"Tonight, we've got a spectacular treat for you all." The excited elves continued to go wild as he spun around on stage in a glittering blue jacket, skillfully building anticipation.

"The team has been working tirelessly behind the scenes to make this our most magical display yet. So, bundle up, hold your loved ones close, and prepare to be dazzled by the most enchanting fireworks display the North Pole has ever seen!"

With a quick signal backstage, someone was coming out to join him. "That's right, folks, the rumours are true. To kick-start tonight's show, it's none other than the magnificent...BRODY CROSBY!"

If Poppy thought the crowd was enthusiastic before, it was nothing compared to the reception that this guy was getting.

"That's the guy from the TV!" Jack said excitedly, "The Ice Hockey player."

It was, and now Poppy looked closer; she could see a lot of elves in the crowd were wearing Crosby shirts. Some even had earmuffs in the shape of hockey pucks.

With unwavering confidence, Brody Crosby took centre stage, greeted by his adoring fans. Waving and smiling, he introduced the show and pressed the grand golden button to release the first fireworks.

In an instant, the night sky burst into a spectacular symphony of colours and lights, illuminating everything around them with breath-taking reds, blues, greens, and golds. The crowd watched in awe as the fireworks danced and sparkled against the backdrop of Santa's cottage.

While everyone gazed upwards, watching the skies, Jack tugged on Poppy's coat. "Look, there's that dreadful woman," he muttered.

Poppy followed his gaze and saw her lurking around at the back of the crowd. It was definitely her. Poppy would recognise that sour expression anywhere.

"If she hates Santa so much, why is she here watching the fireworks at his cottage?" Poppy asked furiously.

"I don't know," Jack said. "She looks suspicious, doesn't she? Like she's up to something."

They squinted to get a better view, but she was standing right at the back, obscured by two male elves.

Instead of watching the fireworks, her gaze was fixed on Santa's cottage as she muttered something under her breath. Suddenly, she turned and locked eyes with Poppy and Jack, her intense stare holding them captive, neither wanting to back down and look away.

Then, out of nowhere, she just walked back towards the trees.

"Okay, that was strange," said Jack, his suspicion at an all-time high. "Come on, let's follow her. I want to know what she's up to."

He spotted the look of hesitation on Poppy's face, "Don't worry, the fireworks will be on for ages. We'll be back before they even notice," he said, gesturing to Wren and Giselle, who were completely captivated by the display.

They followed the mystery elf up the road, back towards The Nutcracker, where she suddenly broke into a run. Confused by how she could have spotted them in the trees, they exchanged puzzled glances, and by the time they looked back, she had vanished entirely.

Approaching cautiously to the spot where they had last seen her, Jack saw a piece of paper on the ground and picked it up, revealing a note inside.

"Meet me behind the Barnaby Wing of the Workshop at 6 a.m. Come alone."

As they stood there, wondering what it was all about, Poppy had an idea.

"The elves she was standing behind at the fireworks, do you think she meant to slip it in one of their pockets? It looked like she was whispering something."

"I don't know," Jack said, unconvinced by Poppy's theory. "Could be, but why would they watch the fireworks if they're like her? Don't they all despise Santa? It doesn't make any sense."

Scanning the area for any other clues, it appeared that the elf had vanished without a trace.

With no other leads, they returned to the fireworks where, as Jack had predicted, no one had even noticed they were gone!

They were just in time for the breath-taking finale, and as the final fireworks went out, the crowd cheered an almighty cheer.

Poppy couldn't understand what was happening at first, but then, in the sky, she saw Santa and Mrs Claus soaring over the North Pole in their sleigh with the reindeer, waving to everyone as they went.

The screen on stage had been transformed to say.

"Merry Christmas, one and all.
See you tomorrow at the Snow Ball."

Poppy forgot all about the elf and the note and stood taking in this unbelievable sight she had dreamed of since she was old enough to learn about Christmas.

Walking back into town with Giselle and Wren afterwards, it seemed like for the first time since they arrived at the North Pole, Giselle was relaxed.

Now, she had seen first-hand that there was no suspicion about Poppy and Jack; she was like a totally different elf! Even cracking jokes! - Bad ones, but jokes nonetheless.

"You two will stay with me again tonight," she said.

"Will we all fit on the snowmobile?" Jack asked, thinking about the squeeze it had been for the three of them today.

"No need," said Giselle. "We'll be getting the Ice Trolley home."

"What's that?" they asked together.
"Err, you call them trains. No, wait, that's not right. A tram! That's it."

Poppy and Jack debated whether to tell Giselle and Wren about the mysterious elf and the note but decided against it. They were both so happy after the fireworks, and Wren had gotten so upset when they spoke about The Opposers before; they didn't want to ruin anyone's night. Especially since they still needed to figure out what they had actually seen. An elf dropping a piece of paper on the floor hardly seemed newsworthy, however strange this woman was.

Poppy thought she'd already witnessed all the jaw-dropping moments the North Pole had to offer, but it had yet another surprise for her as they approached the Ice Trolley. The tram lines were ingeniously built inside a line of giant iridescent baubles, creating the illusion of a magical tunnel.

As Wren waited to see them off, Poppy spotted Mohan heading toward them.

"Surely the Ferris Wheel hasn't gone down again?" Jack teased. "That thing's a liability; remind me not to go on it!"

Poppy laughed, but as Mohan got closer, she sensed the mood changing.

This was something else, something bigger. He whispered something to Wren, who looked shocked.

"Sorry guys, but I'll have to leave you here; they need me back at YuleTrek."

Giselle looked at him to see if everything was okay.

He gave her a slight nod but didn't go into more detail as he sped off with Mohan.

Giselle changed the subject and began telling them how the Ice Trolley worked to avoid any questions.

"It's just two stops on the trolley back to mine," she said. "Each line only has three stops in total: there's the outskirts, where I live; Midtown, where the stables are; and then the centre, which is where we are now. You can go back and forth to the centre from anywhere in the North Pole using the eight different lines around town."

"Like a star!" Poppy said, looking at the map on the wall.

"Exactly!" said Giselle, smiling.

As the tram arrived, it sounded like tiny sleigh bells approaching. Poppy could have listened to that sound all day.

On board, they were greeted with a counter where they could help themselves to hot chocolate and freshly baked cookies. They sat on the long benches with a cookie each and headed off to the outskirts where their day had begun.

Poppy wondered about Wren and if everything was okay at YuleTrek. But these thoughts went out of the window as they passed a huge red building the size of a football stadium.

"What was that!" she asked Giselle.

"That's the North Pole Post Office," she said. "We get millions of letters all year round, not just at Christmas time. In fact, September is particularly busy – lots of people trying to get off the naughty list before Christmas," she chuckled.

"Does it work?" Jack asked curiously.

Giselle laughed, assuming he was joking, but Poppy
sensed he really wanted to know the answer.
"Hey, isn't it the bake-off tomorrow?" asked Poppy.
She had almost forgotten about it after such a big day.
Giselle's face lit up that Poppy had remembered.
"It certainly is," she beamed, "I've been preparing all day.
You'll come, won't you?"
"Absolutely, we wouldn't miss it," they replied.
"So if the bake-off is tomorrow and the Snow Ball is in
the evening, how will you have time to prepare
everything when you win?" Jack asked.
"Oh, you are very kind." Giselle smiled, appreciating his
optimism. "If I win, everything is already prepared. The
team at the Bakery is on standby."

They arrived back at Giselle's and went straight to bed.
Their minds were racing with all the wonderful things
they had seen today. Thanks to Santa's shrinking potion,
tonight they were in real beds with comfortable pyjamas
that Giselle had left out for them, and Poppy was looking
forward to a good night's sleep.
They were so tired, but at the same time, Jack would not
stop speculating about the mysterious elf back at the
fireworks, which carried on (and on) until Poppy finally
drifted off to sleep...

- CHAPTER ELEVEN -

BARNABY'S DIARY

"Poppy, wake up," Jack whispered, gently shaking her. Poppy wasn't sure of the time, but she knew it was far too early to be disturbed.

"What do you want?" she grumbled.

"Something's wrong," he said, sounding worried. "I overheard Giselle on the phone with Wren. I didn't catch all the details, but it sounded like there's a problem at YuleTrek. They've missed a load of houses on Santa's route, and everyone is going crazy trying to fix it before Christmas Eve."

"That can't be right," she said, remembering their conversation with Wren yesterday about the level of planning that went into the YuleTrek operation. "They check and recheck every detail."

"I know, I thought the same. Something feels off." Jack continued. "I'm certain it's connected to that woman."

"Oh, not this again, Jack," Poppy sighed as she flopped back onto her pillow in despair. She was growing tired of Jack's obsession with this woman.

"She's just a hateful, creepy person. There's nothing more to it."

"What about the note?" he insisted.

"It's just a note! People leave notes all the time," Poppy reasoned.

Jack considered his next words carefully before replying. "Prove me wrong then!" he said. "Let's go to the meeting place and see who shows up, and if it's nothing, then I'll shut up about it."

"We don't even know where the Workshop is," Poppy reminded him.

"I do," Jack said, producing a tram map from his bedside table. "I picked this up last night; it's got a full map of the North Pole, including the Workshop."

Poppy took the map off him, slightly impressed by his determination, and studied it more carefully.

The Workshop was on the other side of town from Santa's cottage, where they were last night. It actually was pretty close to the Holly and Ice Market, where the bake-off would take place later today.

"Please, Poppy," he said. "I'm not making a big deal out of nothing here. I really think there's more to this and that this woman is the key," he paused. "You pulled me out of the dog sled that got us here, and now I'm asking you to trust me."

Poppy wasn't sure what he meant by this. Surely he wasn't trying to compare this to the dog sledding - she had been trying to save their lives!

Realising that Jack wasn't going to let this go, she finally relented. "Okay, let's say I agree... what's the plan?" (Knowing full well that he already had one.)

Jack looked delighted, "So, I was thinking we could get the tram into town. We'll leave a note for Giselle that Wren picked us up to help with the reindeer while he is dealing with this Yule Trek stuff, and we will meet her at the bake-off later."

Poppy had to admit it was quite a good plan - deceptive but believable.

"We'll need a pen and paper," she said.

"Already taken care of," he replied with a grin, producing a note from under his pillow.

"I found a notepad on the kitchen fridge - by the way, you have to look in there before we go. There are cakes and cookies everywhere—it looks amazing."

Poppy suddenly felt concerned, "You didn't eat any of it, did you?" she asked suspiciously. "That will all be for the competition."

"No," he laughed, rolling his eyes. "But I did find these." With that, he pulled out two brown paper bags with their names on them from his bedside table.

He was starting to remind Poppy of a magician, the way he kept unveiling hidden items from different hiding spots. Inside the bags were some muffins and cakes that Giselle had set aside for them, which made Poppy feel even more guilty that they were about to deceive her, but if there was any truth to Jack's suspicions, they had to know.

They put the bags into their backpacks, took another dose of shrinking potion, and snuck out to the tram.

The streets were so quiet and peaceful; it was like they had the North Pole to themselves!

On board, they helped themselves to hot chocolate and consulted the map to plan their approach to the Workshop.

It looked like there were plenty of buildings around where they could stay hidden and observe.

In the end, they decided to approach from a street directly behind the Workshop, the furthest from the Holly and Ice market. Remembering that there were two elves they needed to avoid today, the mystery elf and Giselle.

A clock in one of the shop windows told them it was a quarter to six. Poppy couldn't remember the last time she'd been up so early. At weekends, she would lie in until at least ten, and even on school days, she would push her luck until Mr Brown came to drag her out of bed.

They could see the Workshop up ahead, shaped like a giant igloo. Poppy assumed the smaller dome was the Barnaby Wing. It looked much older than the enormous dome that stood ten times the size behind it. There was no entrance to that she could see on this side.

"This must be the back, and you have to go through the main Workshop to get inside the Barnaby Wing," she guessed.

There was nothing to do now but wait, and sure enough, at six o'clock, the elf showed up behind the Barnaby Wing and waited.

She didn't look the same today; yesterday, she looked angry and hateful. Today, she looked concerned - scared even.

"As soon as the others turn up and she is distracted, we'll see if we can get closer," Jack whispered. "We'll sneak up there," he said, pointing to a line of vans parked behind the Workshop.

They waited for someone to join, but after about fifteen minutes, it didn't look like anyone was coming.

The elf looked flustered and darted off in the direction of the vans, where Poppy and Jack lost sight of her.

"Well, that was a bust," Poppy said disappointedly after a few minutes.

"What if she left another note?" Jack suggested, refusing to believe this was it.

They walked over to where she had been standing, but there was no sign of a note. Jack searched under stones and traced the walls with his hands, looking for loose bricks where she could have stashed something, but nothing was there.

"I don't believe it," he said, defeated. "Sorry, Poppy, I was sure -"

"Hello," said a voice behind them.

They spun around, coming face to face with the elf they had been following...

Poppy immediately decided that the best plan was to show no sign they knew who she was.

"Good morning. We were just out for a walk, lovely morning, isn't it?" she said, desperately hoping that the elf didn't recognise them from yesterday.

"I'm glad you came," the elf said, leaving Poppy and Jack baffled. Who did she think they were?

Poppy continued with the "we have no idea who you are" approach.

"Us too. The Workshop is always so beautiful at this time of the morning. Well, have a good day. We'd better get home," Poppy said cheerily, walking away with Jack.

"Don't go!" the woman said.

"Keep moving," Poppy whispered under her breath.

They were just about far enough away to start running when the elf stopped them in their tracks.

"You're not elves, are you?" she said desperately.

They turned to face her, completely caught off guard by her words. How could she possibly know?

"I saw you yesterday - at the carnival," she pointed at Jack. "You were playing with your earmuffs; I saw your ears."

Jack looked horrified. "Are you going to tell anyone?" he said without thinking.

"No," she said thoughtfully, "But I do need your help... that's why I asked you to meet me here."

"Wait, your note was meant for us?" Poppy said, dumbfounded and now feeling pretty sure that they were about to be blackmailed!

Jack was also confused, "But you were so horrible! Why would you do that if you wanted our help? It doesn't make any sense." he said.

"I needed to get your attention," she admitted. "It's complicated to explain. Will you come with me? I want to show you something."

They hesitated, but curiosity got the better of them, and they followed her several metres away from the Workshop to a very ordinary piece of ground.

She stopped and looked at them. Poppy should have trusted her initial instincts; this woman wasn't normal. Was this her big surprise? A pile of snow! She prepared to run away with Jack, but the woman started talking in a language Poppy didn't recognise.

In front of their eyes, the ground moved, revealing an underground passage.

The elf wanted them to go down there with her...

Poppy despaired - why was everyone in the North Pole so obsessed with making her go underground? It was her one fear!

"What's your name?" Poppy asked as if knowing this information would make this any less of a terrible idea.

"Elsie," she said. "Elsie Shadowthorn..." She watched as their concern switched to curiosity. Was she related to Barnaby?

Every sensible part of them told them not to follow her into the passageway, but the news that Elsie was a Shadowthorn had changed everything.

They climbed down, silently walking along as the passage descended deeper underground. Eventually, the tunnel got narrower, and the air grew colder, their breath turning into clouds before them. The walls transitioned from stone to shimmering ice, and the path beneath their feet turned to frosted glass. Poppy wondered how deep they were. She hoped they were getting close, but her heart sank as they discovered a wall of ice blocking their path.

Elsie approached the ice wall and placed her hand on it, whispering something in the same language she used to open the passageway. In response, the wall shuddered and began to melt away, revealing a hidden room with a single chest inside.

"What is this place?" Jack asked, looking around cautiously.

Elsie walked over to the chest. "This is what's left of Barnaby's magic," she replied.

Poppy and Jack stared at the chest for a while. Taking in what Elsie had just said. They had so many questions that needed answering before they could make sense of this situation. Why was she showing this to them? How did she think they could help her? Was this connected to the Aurora Wolves in some way?

Whatever the answers were, Poppy had a bad feeling. "Start at the beginning," she said.

"Why are we here, and why do you need our help...?"

Elsie took a deep breath and sat on the chest. "I assume by now you are familiar with the stories about Barnaby not wanting to share Christmas outside the North Pole?"

Poppy and Jack nodded.

"Barnaby and Santa were great friends. There's no doubt about that," she said. "They spent a lot of time together, and Santa shared tales of his travels around the world and the people he had met. But the more Santa talked about his travels, the more troubled Barnaby became. He heard tales of greed, and selfishness. He could see that humans still had much to learn before they could appreciate Christmas the way the Elves did in the North Pole."

Poppy felt awkward. She didn't like to admit it, but now she had seen the North Pole herself; maybe Barnaby had a point here.

"Barnaby never told Santa his doubts to spare his friend's feelings, but he wrote about them in his diary. Somehow, the diary became known to the other elders and Santa. They confronted Barnaby about his concerns about sharing Christmas with the world."

"What did he say?" Jack asked.

"Barnaby was honest. He told them that, based on what he had heard about the human race, he feared that greed would overshadow the true meaning of Christmas. He worried the meaning would be lost and become about getting stuff and having it all instead of the joy of giving and treasuring time together."

Jack shuffled his feet, and Poppy wondered if, like her, he was thinking about the size of his Christmas list this year.

"The council couldn't understand Barnaby's ideas. It hurt him deeply. He cherished Christmas and just wanted to give people enough time to learn its true meaning."

"So what happened?" Poppy asked.

"The other elders respected Barnaby, and in the end, they agreed to consider his feedback and give them all more time to think. Barnaby went to the outer borders of the North Pole to work on a plan. But when he returned, preparations were already well underway for Santa to leave the North Pole and share Christmas with the world."

"They did it without him?" Jack asked, shocked.

"Not intentionally," Elsie replied. "In the meantime, the council had discussed the idea for the Naughty and Nice list to address Barnaby's concerns. They thought that this way, only people who really appreciated Christmas would receive gifts from the North Pole. They thought that Barnaby would be reassured by this."

"But he wasn't?" Poppy asked.

"No," Elsie said. "Barnaby didn't think the naughty and nice list was the answer. He believed that someone could seem naughty for many reasons but still have a good heart. He didn't want Christmas to be selective; he just wanted the spirit of it to be valued."

"Didn't he say anything?" asked Jack.

Elsie shook her head, "Barnaby was there to help with the first Christmas mission. He'd been so misunderstood before that he didn't want to raise his concerns again. Besides, everyone at the North Pole was so excited and had worked so hard to get Santa ready for his departure. He really hoped that they would prove him wrong."

"But then, why is his magic locked down here?" Poppy asked.

"Even though he didn't say it out loud, he hid some of his magic down here in case they ever needed it after he was gone."

Elsie's voice trailed off, and she began to despair. "But now, The Opposers know about the magic! They want to use it to destroy Christmas, and I need your help to stop them."

They both looked shocked. "How did they even find out about the magic?" Jack asked.

Poppy had been wondering the same.

Elsie looked uncomfortable like she'd been dreading this question. "It was me," she cried, hanging her head in shame.

"A few months ago, I was going through some of my family's old things and found some curious items that led me to this chamber. At the time, I believed in The Opposers view that Barnaby wanted to end Christmas for the outside world. I was honoured to fulfil his wish as his last remaining descendant."

She looked sick.

"But I had overlooked some of the clues, and it wasn't until later I found his diary with the truth."

Poppy couldn't hold back. "Why didn't you just show them the diary then?" she asked, stating the obvious. "Surely they would see they're wrong?"

"I tried!" Elsie cried. "They didn't believe me. They thought it was a fake diary created by Santa to get them to give up on their ideas, but I know it's real. There are things in there about our family that only a Shadowthorn would have known."

Poppy and Jack stared at her. She knew she'd made a mistake, but Poppy wasn't quite ready to let her off the hook yet.

"I'm not sure I get why you were saying nasty things about Santa at the statue to get our attention if you knew the truth. How do you expect us to help you?" Poppy asked.

"Originally, I was going to slip the note in your pocket at the fireworks, but it was so crowded. When I saw you looking at me, I wondered if you might follow me, and you did. Before we could talk, though, I saw something in the trees, like a flash, and it felt like I was being watched, so I vanished and left the note on the ground."

Her voice was getting higher and higher.

"Please, I need your help. I've made too many mistakes in the elf community. No one would take me seriously or listen to me if I tried to tell them the truth. But they might listen to you."

Tears welled up in her eyes, and for the first time, Poppy felt sorry for her.

"I regret joining The Opposers," Elsie said. "I was born into that belief, and I didn't know any different for a very long time. I'll have to explain and make things right with everyone at some point, but right now, I have to protect Christmas, just like Barnaby would have done."

Won over by her story, they were determined to help.

"What do we need to do?" asked Poppy.

"I've been pretending to still go along with The Opposers to learn about their plan," Elsie explained. "They want to use Barnaby's magic to put a curse on the gifts from the North Pole, making every child who plays with them mischievous and bad-tempered. The adults will be so angry that they will never want to receive presents from Santa and the North Pole again."

Poppy couldn't help but look at Jack, feeling guilty that she hadn't taken him more seriously that morning.

"When will they start?" Jack asked urgently.

"Today," Elsie replied. "In fact, they're meeting right now to finalise everything. I was able to excuse myself by telling Mordane that I thought we could make the magic more powerful with some treasures from my ancestors, but we don't have much time."

"Who's Mordane?" Poppy asked.

"Mordane is the leader of The Opposers. His family has been against Santa for as long as anyone can remember. His ancestor, Felix Frostshade, wanted to manage the Workshop when it first expanded, but he lost out to another elf and couldn't let it go. He became bitter and troublesome, playing pranks on the other elves and Santa, which got more and more dangerous. He was the first (and last) elf ever to be put on the naughty list, and his whole family has despised Santa ever since."

Elsie checked her watch. "We must hurry. I can answer more questions later, but if you're willing to help me, we need to move. I saw you with Wren last night; he works at YuleTrek, doesn't he?"

Poppy and Jack nodded.

"So, you might've already guessed that they've started putting their plan in motion. There's an Opposer inside YuleTrek. Last night, while everyone was at the fireworks, they messed with Santa's Christmas Eve route. The Opposers want to deliver extra presents to grandparents', aunts, and uncles' houses where children might be visiting for Christmas Day to make sure the damage hits as hard and as quickly as possible. Tonight, during the Snow Ball, they plan to break into the Workshop and curse all of the gifts."

"We have to tell Wren!" Jack said urgently. "He's at YuleTrek now with the others. They think it's something they did wrong!" he looked so upset for his friend.

"We don't have much time," Poppy said. "Let's work on a plan."

Elsie looked at them both with a soft voice and teary eyes. "Thank you for believing me," she whispered. "I was beginning to think I'd have to face this alone."

- CHAPTER TWELVE -

THE OPPOSERS

Meanwhile, in Barnaby's cabin beyond the borders of the North Pole, a sinister plan was taking shape.

A group of rebellious elves had gathered, their hearts full of bitterness, making their final preparations to stop Christmas in the outside world once and for all.

"Darrian, Bramma, Morgana, and Thorne," a commanding voice barked through the dimly lit room, "You'll be our eyes and ears at the Snow Ball tonight. We need to know what Santa and his top elves are up to at all times. If anything seems off or if they get a hint of our plans, contact Elara. She'll coordinate our actions from here and alert the others."

Elara, a surprisingly tall elf with a twisted grin that never seemed to leave her face, sat at the back of the room. Her laugh sent shivers down the spines of those unfortunate enough to hear it, and she looked delighted, knowing that Santa was on the edge of his downfall. The voice continued, "Soren, Morgrim, and Ravenna, "Westley will leave the Workshop unlocked tonight. You'll get Barnaby's magic from the chamber and place it inside the Barnaby Wing. Wait for us there. Elsie, Kalethorn, and I will be there at nine-thirty exactly to cast the curse on the gifts before they start loading the sleigh tomorrow."

"Now, everyone, carry on with your day as usual," the voice urged. "No one can suspect a thing. If anyone has questions, speak now, as this is our final meeting before tonight. There can be no mistakes."

The room fell into a heavy silence, each elf fully aware of their role in this dark plot.

Just as Mordane was about to move on, there was a question.

"What about Elsie?" asked Elara, her chilling voice echoing from the back of the room. "I mean, she's not even here. Are you sure she's up to this?"

Mordane paused, and the room tensed.

"Your questioning of my judgement will not be tolerated, Elara," he warned. "Elsie is on a private mission for me right now. As a direct descendant of Barnaby, her connection to magic is stronger than any of us. It's true that she briefly wavered in her commitment to this cause after finding the diary, but since learning it was a fake, she's more determined than ever to see this plan through."

"Does anybody else have any questions or doubts that they'd like to share?" he hissed, not really expecting anyone to answer. "Elsie has as much to prove tonight as any of us. Santa made a fool of her with that fake diary. We've been ridiculed, overlooked, and criticized for years by those blindly following Santa, but tonight, our voices will be heard. They underestimate our numbers and how deeply we've infiltrated their lives."

The room buzzed with anger and a sense of justice as the elves prepared for their dark mission.

"Tonight, we take back what's rightfully ours. Christmas belongs to the North Pole; it was born here, and it will stay here forever. That imposter with the white beard will have nothing left by the end of the week, and we will all have front-row seats to witness his undoing."
The room erupted into a chilling cheer as they prepared to set the final parts of their plan in motion...

- CHAPTER THIRTEEN -

YULETREK

Back in the underground chamber, Poppy, Jack, and Elsie had finished finalising their plans to stop The Opposers.

Poppy and Jack would take the tram to the stables to warn Wren. Meanwhile, Elsie would continue undercover with The Opposers to avoid suspicion. She gave them a list with the names of all The Opposers and where they'd be tonight. Poppy couldn't believe what she was reading. They had elves inside Workshop, the Post Office, and YuleTrek, all plotting to betray their friends. She knew she could never do something like that.

They left the underground chamber, and Poppy and Jack headed for the tram station. As they crossed the town, everything felt strangely normal. On the surface, people were busy with their daily routines, blissfully unaware of the extraordinary events that had just unfolded beneath them.

The town squares had undergone a magical transformation overnight; colourful banners and signs celebrating the day's two major events, the highly anticipated bake-off and the enchanting Snow Ball, were hung on every available surface.

The smell of freshly baked goods wafted through the air as bakers prepared their most mouth-watering creations, all hoping for the title of "North Pole Baking Champion."

Seeing everyone so joyful, embracing their beautiful culture and traditions, only made Poppy and Jack more determined to protect them.

They boarded the next tram, headed for midtown, with their sights set on the stables and YuleTrek headquarters.

The winding track up to the airfield and the walk to the stables felt never-ending today.

"Wren said there were common areas where everyone met; maybe we will find him there?" Jack suggested as they walked past the reindeer. They were desperate to say hello, but they were all napping.

"Lazy bunch, aren't they." Jack laughed. "Mind you, if I had to fly around the world in a few days, I'd probably need some rest too."

Continuing on their way, they approached another building. Cautiously, they peered through the window, but the room was empty, with only a few sofas and a TV inside. They moved along to try another building.

"Jack, I think we're going the wrong way," Poppy said, pointing in the opposite direction. In the distance, they could see the tip of the YuleTrek logo, the same symbol they had seen in Wren's apartment.

They headed through the maze of small buildings and finally reached YuleTrek headquarters, where the YuleTrek logo was proudly displayed above the doors. Entering reception, they found a young elf behind the desk with his back to them. He seemed flustered, flipping through several files on top of a sideboard.

They waited for a moment, but he didn't seem to notice them.

Poppy cleared her throat. "Excuse me, we're looking for…" She suddenly realised she had no idea what Wren's surname was, so she just said "Wren" and left it there, hoping that there wasn't more than one Wren at YuleTrek.

The receptionist finally turned to face them. "Sorry, everyone's swamped right now," he replied. "There's no time for meetings today; you'll have to come back after Christmas."

With that, he turned back to his files.

"It's urgent," Jack insisted. "Very urgent, actually."

The elf turned around again, looking slightly annoyed now. "I'm sorry, but as I said, everyone's very busy today. I'm sure whatever it is can wait. YuleTrek doesn't need the help of two children. Shouldn't you two be out enjoying the carnival anyway?"

Realising that they wouldn't get a meeting with Wren this way, they headed back outside.

"We need a distraction," Poppy said. "He's the only one in there. If we can distract him, we can easily slip past." Jack's face suddenly lit up with an idea. "The reindeer!" he said. "I bet Rudolph will help us. We can lead him out here so the receptionist thinks he got out, and while they take him back to the stables, we can sneak inside."

"Brilliant!" said Poppy. They hurried down to the stables, where the reindeer were still peacefully napping.

"I feel awful waking him," Poppy said. "Let's get a carrot with icing sugar and see if he smells it."

Sure enough, by the time they turned around, Rudolph was awake. He recognised them right away and came over, giving them a friendly nudge.

"Hello, boy," said Jack, gently stroking his neck. "Sorry to wake you, but we need your help."

They opened the stall door, unsure if Rudolph would follow them. At first, he just stood there, but Poppy grabbed some more carrots off the side and lured him towards the reception area.

They put him in view of the doors, giving him a final carrot to keep him busy while they hid behind the stairs. Jack picked up a stone and tossed it at the door to get the receptionist's attention.

"Rudolph!" they heard him cry. "How did you get out?" The receptionist hurried out of the building, looking confused. Realising no one was there, he laughed. "I see you've helped yourself to some carrots, too."

As they heard him leading Rudolph off back to the stables, they ran into the building. "Let's go," Poppy whispered as they headed for the corridor behind the reception desk, where they found a lift.

Ground Floor
Reception and Breakout
Floor One
Administration
Floor Two
Research and Development
Floor Three
Command Centre
Floor Four
Santa's office and Leadership

It's got to be on the third floor, do you think? Let's give it a try," said Poppy.

They pressed the button for the third floor, and as the doors gave a cheerful "ping," they quickly discussed their approach.

"Let's try to get Wren's attention without anyone noticing," Poppy whispered to Jack, who nodded in agreement.

"Third floor," the lift announced as the doors opened. Suddenly, their plans for a low-key entrance unravelled before their eyes. The doors had directly opened into the command room, where no fewer than twelve very confused elves were staring straight at them…

Among the sea of confused faces, they spotted Wren, who was just as baffled as everyone else to see them.

"Let's take a short break," he announced loudly, walking towards Poppy and Jack.

"Guys, what are you doing here?" he whispered.

"We need to talk to you," Poppy blurted out in panic Wren's expression changed, sensing that this must be important. He ushered them back into the lift and pressed the button for the fourth floor.

"What about Santa?" Jack asked, worried.

"Santa isn't here; he's preparing for the Snow Ball with Mrs Claus," Wren said.

Exiting the lift, they walked down the corridor to Wren's office, peeking into other offices along the way.

At the end of the hallway was a big wooden door with the words "Merry Christmas One and All" painted on the front; there was no doubt whose office that was.

Wren showed them into his surprisingly neat office. He had a small Christmas tree on his desk, complete with reindeer decorations, one for each of Santa's reindeer. In the corner of the room was a cosy fireplace, and on the bookshelves were jars of sweets and a collection of antique maps and compasses. He closed the door behind them and took a seat.

"What's going on?" he asked seriously. "Why are you here at YuleTrek?"

They told him the entire story, starting with the note they found at the fireworks, leaving Giselle's house this morning to meet Elsie, and the information about The Opposers plan.

Wren's face dropped as they spoke; he couldn't believe it. They gave him the list of The Opposers and their locations this evening. For several minutes, he sat in shock, trying to process everything.

A few times, he went to say something but then stopped. Eventually, he started pacing around the room.

"This can't be right. My team is solid. There's no way anyone would be involved in something like this. And the Workshop... I've known those guys for years. These names can't be right..."

Poppy and Jack watched him. Wren was having a hard time believing that any of the elves at the North Pole could be so deceitful.

"We're just sharing what we heard," Poppy said gently. "I know it's hard to accept, but remember, just yesterday, we thought Aurora wolves were extinct, and now we've seen three of them. Things aren't always as they seem."

As she said this, Poppy's mind suddenly connected the dots on something Elsie had said about seeing a flash of light in the trees and feeling like she was being watched. "Wren, I think there might have been Aurora Wolves at the fireworks last night," she said, surprising even herself with these words.

Jack also looked shocked about where this sudden information had come from.

"I kept thinking yesterday in the caves, there must be a reason they've appeared. Do you think it's possible they've returned to help protect the North Pole from The Opposers?"

Wren fell silent again, searching for an alternative explanation, but he couldn't escape the reality that Poppy's theory might hold some truth.

Suddenly, Wren sprang into action. "The only way to be sure of any of this is to let this play out," he said. "This could still be a trick set up by The Opposers, and if not, then tonight is when people will reveal their true colours." Poppy and Jack agreed.

"Until then, we must go about our day normally as if nothing has happened."

Poppy felt relieved that Wren was starting to come around and believe their story.

"What time is it now?" he asked.

"Ten-thirty," Poppy replied.

"Alright, here's what we're going to do," he said.

- CHAPTER FOURTEEN -

THE NORTH POLE BAKE-OFF

They agreed that Wren would keep YuleTrek working on the fake problem to avoid suspicion from The Opposers. At the same time, behind the scenes, he and Mohan would work on restoring the original Christmas Eve route.

To explain Poppy and Jack's sudden appearance at YuleTrek, they'd stick to their original story – that Poppy and Jack were helping with the reindeer and Rudolph's escape had been the reason for their urgent interruption. Wren was going to visit Santa soon to update him on the YuleTrek situation. During that meeting, he would share the entire story, including his and Giselle's temporary departure from the North Pole and the arrival of Poppy and Jack. This had everyone feeling a bit nervous.

Poppy and Jack were to go to the bake-off to support Giselle. When it was finished, they would tell her everything before meeting at the Snow Ball at six-thirty that evening. There was no time to waste.

Poppy and Jack hopped on the tram to return to the town centre. It was just as busy as last night for the fireworks. They weaved through the crowds and arrived at the Holly and Ice Market, which was packed full of handcrafted treasures.

They discovered everything from decorations, Christmas cards, and stationery to pottery, hats, and music boxes. Large 3D sculptures hung above every stall as giant replicas of the wonderful items on offer.

Following the signs for the bake-off, they were amazed to find a life-sized gingerbread house at the entrance. Its golden brown walls baked to perfection and held together with bright white icing made to look like snow. Icicles crafted from sugar dangled from the edible roof, and the front door was made from a giant slab of chocolate.

As they continued through the gingerbread house, the smell was incredible. The living room was also completely edible, with icing paintings on the walls, a dining room table made from an enormous chocolate chip cookie, a TV made of liquorice, and even a chandelier cleverly constructed from jelly beans.

Heading into the garden, they found a candy cane archway covered in sparkling lights and a cheerful elf who stood waiting to greet everyone.

"Welcome to the North Pole Bake-off!" she exclaimed, handing them a chocolate bar with a message inscribed on it. "Come right this way," she said as she ushered them under the archway.

Jack peered over Poppy's shoulder. "What does it say?" he asked as Poppy read it out loud.

"As the maze gently winds, and you find your way through.
You'll emerge at the bake-off with the grandest of views."

"A maze?" Jack's face lit up with excitement.
"It must be this way," said Poppy, looking up ahead.

The path inside the maze was made from soft, fluffy marshmallows where they could race and bounce along. Dead ends were guarded by giant gummy bears, and the hedges were lined with lollipops and chocolate-covered fruit trees.

They happily bounced their way through the maze and eventually reached the entrance to the bake-off stadium. Inside, eight large benches were arranged in the centre, with signs displaying the contestants' names and the North Pole bakeries they represented.

Iris Freeman - Sleigh Bell Sweets
Giselle Frostblossom - Sugar and Snowflake Bakery
Ryan Willowglen - Tinsel and Treats
Hazel Chapman - Jingle Bell Bakes
Freddie Emberstone - Candy Cane Confections
Macey Goldengrove - The Milk and Cookie Company
Lyla Twinkletree — Polar Patisserie
Callum Jinglewood — The Snow Shack

Spotting Giselle, they waved and cheered to get her attention before finding their seats. Her face lit up when she saw them. She was surrounded by the same amazing cakes and cookies they'd seen in her kitchen earlier. Poppy expected Giselle to look nervous from the way she had talked so far about the bake-off, but actually, she looked the total opposite. Entirely at home, surrounded by her baking and ready to start the competition.

From what Poppy could tell, there'd be four rounds, and it looked like they could walk around with the judges while the bake-off was taking place to test out some of the treats provided by each contestant.

There were four judges, and if they couldn't agree on a winner, the audience would have the final vote.

The stylish host introduced the bakers, and the judges began moving around from station to station with their clipboards as the crowd joined them.

The first round was called "Decorator's Delight." Giselle set up her station, bringing out a miniature Christmas tree, and began to create beautifully decorated biscuit ornaments to hang off it. Hazel from Jingle Bell Bakes made a whole family of sharply dressed snowmen from cupcakes, while the contestant from The Snow Shack decorated a giant cookie to look like a festive patchwork jumper.

Jack couldn't resist heading over to Candy Cane Confections to sample some of the flavours he'd been desperate to try the night before in the shop window. Despite the crowds buzzing around them, the contestants stayed totally focused as the competition tested their skills. After each round, everyone returned to their seats to cast their votes, which would be counted and revealed at the end.

The next round was "Chocolate Delights". Poppy jumped out of her skin in surprise as the stadium came to life and began to move. The contestant benches were now separated by a river of chocolate, and an impressive chocolate waterfall cascaded from the back of the stage, feeding the river.

Christmas trees emerged from the stage, studded with fruit, pretzels, marshmallows, and other bite-sized treats that the audience could dunk in the waterfall, like the world's largest chocolate fountain!

Once again, the bakers displayed their creativity, crafting bouquets of delicate flowers, volcanos with flowing chocolate lava," and a life-size chocolate reindeer. But Giselle stole the show in this round with a giant chocolate dragon that impressed everyone. Each scale on its body was carved to perfection, and she even used dry ice to make smoke come out of its nostrils.

The "Secret Ingredient Challenge" was up next, presenting a challenging twist for the contestants.

Each one was given a peculiar ingredient to include in their design. Giselle was given a dragon fruit in honour of the previous round, while the rest received other strange ingredients like smoked salt, black garlic, wasabi, dandelion, and blue cheese. While they worked on their creations, the audience took part in a blind taste test, trying to guess the mystery flavours hidden inside various brownies and cakes. Jack refused to try anymore after realising he had eaten a sweetcorn-flavoured brownie, and Poppy also had a strange one that tasted like vinegar.

Excitement escalated as they approached the final round, where the bakers would present their most spectacular, festive centrepieces fit for a Christmas Day feast.

Giselle got to work on a remarkable ice castle made from sponge cake and melted sweets. She lit it up with fairy lights to make it sparkle like the Northern Lights.

There were charming gingerbread villages and other edible Christmas scenes - one even made a snow globe cake with white chocolate suspended in jelly, making it look like it had just been shaken.

When the final round was complete, everyone returned to their seats, awaiting the judges' final results. Poppy saw nerves on Giselle's face for the first time.

The host announced that the judges had all agreed on a winner.

"And the Winner is...Giselle Frostblossom! From the Sugar and Snowflake Bakery! For her incredible use of colour and craftsmanship in her lifelike chocolate dragon."

Poppy and Jack cheered at the top of their lungs, beaming with pride for their friend and probably also experiencing a sugar rush.

Giselle looked so happy. She received a massive bouquet of flowers and a golden winner's trophy. She thanked her bakery team and shared details with the crowd about the treats and confections they could expect tonight at the Snow Ball.

As the crowd rushed to congratulate Giselle, Poppy couldn't help but think about the horrible information they had to share with her next. It seemed so unfair after her fantastic win, but in the end, Giselle already knew something was wrong.

As soon as the crowd surrounding her died down, she headed over to them, looking concerned. "What's wrong?" she said. "Something's happened; I know it has. There's no way Wren would have missed this if it wasn't important."

They found a quiet spot in the stadium and explained the whole story...

Giselle's face, like Wren's, went through a whirlwind of emotions – from shock to anger, then sadness.

Poppy wasn't sure how Giselle would take the news that Wren had decided to tell Santa about their secret return to the North Pole, but she completely understood.

"Right," she said, gathering her thoughts. "There's only one thing left to do then." Poppy and Jack leaned in, waiting for her answer. "We need to get you two ready for the Snow Ball! Excuse me, I need to make a quick call," she said, walking away.

- CHAPTER FIFTEEN -

THE SNOW BALL

Poppy thought they'd catch the tram back to Giselle's house, but they walked right past it.

"Where are we going?" Jack asked.

"You'll see," Giselle smiled.

They kept walking until they reached a grand street with several antique and fine jewellery shops. In the middle was a very elegant suit shop.

"Here we are," Giselle said, inviting them inside the shop called "Silver Stitch".

The shop was empty except for an elderly elf who welcomed Giselle with open arms. "Giselle, my dear! Congratulations on your win. We're all so proud," he said. "I'm so sorry I couldn't be there in person. It's been such a busy morning with everyone getting ready for the Snow Ball tonight. But I watched the whole thing on TV; you were brilliant. Your mother and grandfather would be so proud."

Giselle gave the elf a big hug. "Poppy, Jack, I want you to meet my uncle - Rufus Silverstitch, the finest tailor in all of the North Pole!"

The elf looked very happy with this compliment. "So, this is the famous Poppy and Jack?" he asked, giving them a kind smile. "And we need an Elvin tailcoat for Jack, is that right?"

"Yeah, please," said Giselle. "Sorry again for the short notice."

"No problem at all, my dear. We'll find something. Jack, pop your coat on the chair for me and come stand on this step," he said, reaching for his tape measure. "Now, what colour are your eyes?" he said, looking at Jack's face as he measured him. "Ah, Hazel. The colour of those that possess great creativity."

Rufus went over to the racks on the other side of the room and pulled out three velvet tailcoats in green, navy, and red. "Let's try this red one first," he said, handing it to Jack. "See how you feel," he added as he made some minor adjustments and pointed to the mirror.

The top of the jacket was fitted, and it flared out into a dramatic, flowing tail at the back. Poppy could tell right away that Jack wasn't a fan of the white lace on the cuffs and collar. "Hmm, it's okay. Could we try the green one?" Jack asked, hoping he wouldn't hurt Rufus's feelings.

"Of course," Rufus replied with a smile. "You have to be confident in what you wear. Elvin Tails are a reflection of the elf who wears them. The green jacket looked lovely, a deep emerald green with gathered satin instead of lace on the cuffs and collar. There were snowflakes embroidered down the sides, and gold snowflake buttons lined the front. Poppy liked it way better than the red one.

"I love it," said Jack proudly, looking at himself from all angles in the mirror.

"Wonderful!" said the elf. "Let's try these trousers and boots, and then we'll find you a hat."

Jack suddenly looked panicked. He looked to Giselle, who realised he was worrying about removing his earmuffs. "It's okay. He knows everything," she said warmly.

Jack relaxed. "Yes, we'll need a hat that covers your ears well. I'll check what we have," Rufus said, heading out to the back of the shop.

While Jack looked through the other jackets in the shop, Giselle came over to talk to Poppy. "I hope you don't mind, but I have something at home that I think will be perfect for you," she said, hoping Poppy wouldn't mind not having something new to wear to the Snow Ball, like Jack. "It was my mother's prom dress," she said softly. "I wore it to my first Snow Ball, too." Poppy was touched. "I'd be absolutely honoured," she said as Rufus returned with a selection of hats.

With Jack all set, Rufus packed up his new clothes and bid them farewell as they headed back to the tram stop. On the ride back, more well-wishers came over to congratulate Giselle, and a question that Poppy had been meaning to ask since they arrived popped into her head. "Giselle, what recipe were you and Wren looking for when we met?" Giselle smiled. "Have you ever heard of Kalaallit Kaagiat?" Poppy shook her head, unsure if she could even say it, let alone have tried it.

"It's somewhere between a cake and bread. It's a traditional dish in Greenland, much less sweet than the cakes we're used to in the North Pole," she explained.

"I read about it in a book my Grandfather had when I was little, and I'd always been curious to try it, but I never found the recipe. Anyway, Wren convinced me I should make it in the competition this year to honour my grandfather, so that's why we were out searching for it." Poppy felt terrible - they were the reason Giselle never found her recipe. "We're so sorry, Giselle," she said.

"Sorry!" Giselle said. "Whatever for, you have nothing to apologise for. The universe clearly had other plans for us that day - or maybe it was the North Pole telling me that they aren't ready to give up on sugar just yet," she chuckled.

"Besides, it didn't hurt my chances in the completion anyway, did it?" She winked, holding up her winner's trophy.

Back inside Giselle's cosy house, they had about two hours before they had to meet Wren at the Snow Ball. Giselle decided to make one final check at the bakery before the Snow Ball, so she dropped her things off and left Poppy and Jack to start getting ready. She put her mother's dress in the guest room for Poppy, who couldn't resist trying it on.

It was an unusual but stunning dress, ice blue with silver mesh and delicate embroidery. The bottom puffed out like a princess dress, with white feathers sewn into the fabric, creating a soft and fluffy ending. Giselle had also left out a selection of traditional beaded necklaces and a sparkling vine tiara with blue crystals for Poppy to wear with it. It made her excited to see what everyone else would be wearing tonight.

They finally got Jack's hair under control so his hat didn't keep slipping off, and they were ready.

Giselle arrived back from the bakery. Her hair doubled in size, but everything was under control for the ball, and she rushed off to get ready.

They waited in the living room until she emerged in a stunning white dress with pink and purple ruffles around the waist and long lace sleeves. She had a star-like tiara and a selection of beaded necklaces and bracelets. She looked wonderful.

"Okay, are we ready for the ball?" she asked. "Let's go and bring these Opposers to justice once and for all, shall we?"

They looked at her, feeling both determined and nervous and ready to face whatever was coming as they set off into town.

The Snow Ball was a grand and glittering affair held in a glass-roofed ballroom not too far from the Workshop. As they approached the building, a brass band was there to greet everyone, glowing under the lights of brightly lit Christmas trees that lined the red carpet.

Inside the domed hall, the walls sparkled with icicles and evergreen garlands. In one corner stood an enormous Christmas tree, decked out with shiny ornaments and twinkling lights. The elves were all dressed in their finest clothes, a festival of shimmering gowns, showy tailcoats, and fancy headwear. The music was lively, and the dance floor was full of elves spinning and twirling.

"Let's get a drink," Giselle suggested, shouting over the noise and leading them over to a giant brass contraption filled with ice. Taps poked out from all sides, offering a huge selection of Christmas drinks, from Hot Chocolate to Eggnog, Mulled Wine, Peppermint Punch, Gingerbread Latte, and Spiced apple cider. They poured themselves a Pomegranate Lemonade and stood sipping it while taking in the rest of the room.

In the middle of the domed ceiling hung a giant chandelier loaded with flickering candles and winter garland. Lanterns were placed on the tables surrounding the dance floor, filled with greenery and twinkling lights.

The band, called "Avalanche," played lively, festive rock music, much to the surprise of Poppy and Jack, who were really enjoying the music.

Giselle finally spotted Wren across the room and waved him over.

As he came over, he was beaming. "Congratulations on the win! Incredible, just incredible," he said as he approached, giving Giselle a massive hug.

"I'm so sorry I couldn't be there. It's been such a disaster today with all this stuff at YuleTrek, but it's all sorted now. We're back on track for Christmas Eve," he beamed.

"That's wonderful," Giselle said.

Jack was about to open his mouth, presumably to ask questions about the plan, but Wren cut him off before he could get the words out.

"Well, excuse me, I need to go and say hello to some people, but I'll be back soon; we need to talk about that chocolate dragon! Absolutely inspired!" he said, walking away.

Of course, Poppy had not been expecting him to go into the full details of everything right there, but some update or information would have been nice. She and Jack both felt a little confused, but Giselle was looking at them; she obviously knew something they didn't.

"Oh look, a photo booth," she said. "How fun! Shall we have a look?"

They went to the photo booth and bundled into the small cubicle, where Giselle signalled them to stay quiet.

From the ruffles of her dress, she produced a note that Wren must have put there when he hugged her. She held it up so they could all see:

"Eyes everywhere, not safe to talk out loud.
The Opposers are monitoring Snow Ball inside and out.
Giselle, I need you to create a BIG distraction at 9:28 pm exactly.
Mohan will use this to slip out to Barnaby's Cabin and disable Elara.
We must make sure she makes her final announcement before we ambush The Opposers. Once she has given Mordane and the others the "go" to move on the Workshop. That's when we strike.
We ambush all Opposers at the Snow Ball at 9:30 pm.
Giselle, your target is Bramma; don't let him out of your sight.

Poppy and Jack — You're our secret weapon. The Opposers don't know about you. You're the only ones they're not tracking.
Get to the Workshop and slow them down until we can capture the others and meet you there.
Do whatever it takes.
Santa and the North Pole are counting on you.
PS: There's a bag under the Christmas Dinner buffet table - take it with you."

Poppy took the note from Giselle and turned it over, expecting to find more information on the back. That couldn't be it, could it?

"Poppy and Jack, slow them down, good luck."

That's not a plan; it's barely even a note!

Realising that the fate of the North Pole now rested largely on their shoulders, she felt quite queasy. They had to slow down not one but six Opposers! Okay, one of them was on their side, but still! There'd better be something really good in this mystery bag!

Unable to voice her concerns and aware of the time they'd spent in the photo booth, they took a few silly photos and returned outside, laughing like nothing had happened.

Giselle excused herself to the little elves' room, and suddenly, despite being in a very crowded room, they felt alone.

"Want to get some food?" Jack suggested, following Wren's instruction, to retrieve the bag.

As they approached the buffet tables, they faced their first challenge: the Christmas Dinner table was enormous! How were they going to search for the bag without it looking suspicious?

The food, though, looked incredible, a Christmas feast, complete with all the trimmings. They couldn't resist quickly grabbing a plate, loading it with mouth-watering turkey, roast potatoes, stuffing, and vegetables.

As they ate, they admired the incredible dessert table with all of Giselle's marvellous creations; they all looked too beautiful to eat. There were Penguin shaped truffles, Igloo cupcakes, Snowman s'mores, Santa Hat cake pops, and more, as well as a table showcasing the spellbinding centrepieces created by the bake-off contestants; Giselle's stood proudly on the winner's stand.

"What do you think?" Poppy asked after they finished eating. "We need to get under the table without being noticed. Any ideas?"

"I've got something; follow my lead," Jack said, walking over to a group of younger elves. "Tag, you're it!" he shouted, tagging one of them on the shoulder.

They looked at him, confused at first, but then they all started racing around, trying to tag each other, with Jack joining in. One of the elves was trying particularly hard to catch Jack, and he dived under the table to escape them, coming out at the opposite end with the bag in his hands! He continued racing around with them, but by now, they were causing quite a scene at the buffet.

"Sienna, Celeste, if you and the others want to run around, why don't you go outside where there's more space?" said one of the parents.

That was their signal. "Alright, everyone, last one out is a glass of rotten eggnog!" yelled Jack as the young elves raced towards the door. On the way, they bumped into a suspicious-looking elf hovering around the entrance that Poppy suspected was an Opposer on watch. He barely registered the rush of children running outside to play except for grumbling about "stupid kids."

They left the others playing and headed for the shelter of some nearby trees. "How did you come up with that?" Poppy said. "Brilliant, totally brilliant!"

Jack laughed, "You can always count on adults to stop you running indoors. Mum and Dad are always sending me outside," he said as they walked further up the path.

"What's next?" he asked, his adrenaline pumping.

"Well, I'm hoping there's another note or something in this bag," said Poppy, taking it off Jack's shoulder and peering inside. To her disappointment, there was no note. In fact, she wasn't quite sure what it was!

"Isn't that the Tinsel Twirler Five Hundred from Wren's apartment?" Jack asked. "What are we supposed to do with that?"

As Jack said these words, Poppy suddenly understood the message from Wren and smiled.

"We do whatever it takes," she said. "Just like the note said."

Jack grinned as he also caught onto what Wren and Santa were giving them permission to do.

"Let's go and show these Opposers they can't mess with Christmas and get away with it," Poppy declared as they headed toward the Workshop.

- CHAPTER SIXTEEN -

THE WORKSHOP

So far, they'd been behind and underneath the Workshop but not inside. They followed their way around from the back of the Barnaby wing to the front doors, where two giant nutcrackers stood on either side of the golden doors. An enormous mallet hung above the entrance, hammering up and down. The door was slightly open.

"They look like fresh footprints," said Poppy, pointing in the snow. "Someone's already been here."

They snuck inside, leaving the door in the same position as they found it, and looked around to see if anyone was there. It was so hard not to make a sound when all they wanted to do was scream in excitement at what they could see. The Workshop was everything Poppy had ever imagined and more. Wooden workstations with tool boxes and wrapping paper strewn across them, a conveyor belt that wove in and out between the stations to move gifts from one area to another. On the wall hung a countdown clock, showing the days, hours, and minutes left until the big day. There was colour and joy everywhere they looked.

They spotted a staircase leading up to a balcony and what looked like an apartment rather than an office with the name Esme Carolwood - Workshop Manager, carved on the front door.

"Is that a train track?" Jack whispered excitedly. Poppy followed the tracks with her eyes to the very back of the enormous room, where an emerald green train with several carts attached displayed the name "Managers Express" on the front.

There was an entire section of the Workshop dedicated to gift wrapping and a huge Wrapping Paper Printing Press where the elves could design and print their own wrapping paper! Alongside it was the widest selection of bows, ribbons, gift tags, stickers, twine, bells, and stamps that Poppy had ever seen.

"What's that over there, do you think?" Poppy said quietly, walking over to something that looked like an indoor assault course.

"Quality testing," Jack read softly from one of the signs. The space was filled with trampolines, towering slides, obstacle courses, and balconies of different heights. All equipped with toys to put through their paces to test their quality and sturdiness. Poppy knew that if Jack could choose any job in the North Pole, this would be it - a Toy Tester!

"We need to find the Barnaby Wing," she whispered, prising Jack away from the testing station. "It must be down there."

She pointed to a tunnel-like corridor, and with bated breath, they crept along to the Barnaby Wing. Crouching behind the door at the end and looking through the small gap, they could just about see what was happening inside. Along the back wall were three objects suspended in golden light. A stocking, a mallet, and a rocking horse – "The Enchanted Trinity!"

The stocking was made from rich red velvet with shimmering threads of platinum and a perfect white cuff. The mallet, with its head of enchanted silver, engraved with toys, candy canes, and wrapped gifts. And finally, the rocking horse of flight, with a flowing mane of gold and wings sculpted from clouds; they were the most beautiful objects that Poppy had ever seen!

There were three figures in the room. All dressed in purple, hooded cloaks, walking around the outside of a gigantic hole in the floor filled with presents.

"How many extra gifts do you think they had to make today just so we can curse them?" one of them sneered.

"This time next year, this present chute will just be a forgotten hole in the ground," said another as they cackled together.

"We'd better sit down; Elara will be giving another update soon. Santa's at the Snow Ball now. Everything's going to plan; the others should be here within the hour." The group made their way toward the armchairs near the fireplace in the room, awaiting further instructions.

Poppy and Jack crept back up the tunnel and returned to the main Workshop.

"We don't have long; let's get to work," said Poppy, handing Jack some overalls she'd found near the front door. They shared some ideas and began laying out their surprises, awaiting the arrival of the final Opposers...

With ten minutes to spare until 9:30 pm, they hid in the train carts at the back of the room.

Elsie, Kalethorn, and Mordane wouldn't be long now. Poppy couldn't help but wonder how Elsie must be feeling. It was the first time she'd thought about her properly since this morning. There'd been so much going on today; they'd mostly been running on adrenaline until now.

Crouched in the tiny train cart, she suddenly felt nervous. Was everyone's piece of the puzzle going to plan? Were they going to be able to pull this off? She could tell Jack was thinking the same. Thankfully, they didn't have long to linger on these thoughts as the door to the Workshop creaked, and Elsie appeared, followed by the other two. Poppy tried to work out who was who.

One was a red-haired elf with a round face and sunken eyes, while the other seemed like they'd never had a joyful day in their life. Like they spent all their time being thoroughly unimpressed by everyone and everything they encountered. Poppy decided this must be Mordane.

"Changed a bit, hasn't it?" said the elf, which Poppy assumed was Kalethorn.

"It's an abomination," said the other sharply. "But not for much longer. Soon, it will be a forgotten shack that went out of business."

"I'll take this in the closing down sale," Elsie laughed, picking up a toy polar bear as the others joined her in a spiteful cackle.

Her laugh sent a shudder down Poppy's spine, and she was instantly reminded of their first awful encounter with Elsie. Upon hearing the laughter, the other elves approached from the Barnaby Wing.

"We thought we heard you; what's so funny?" they asked.

"Elsie was just making her wish list for Santa's closing down sale," said Mordane as the laughter started up again. Mordane, who'd now clearly had enough of the joke, turned back to a more serious tone. "Is it here?" he asked.

"Yes, it's in the other room," one of the others said.

"Good, let's get moving then; there's no time to waste." Poppy saw Elsie hold herself back, looking around the room for clues about what was coming next, but it was too risky to communicate with her.

As the elves left the main Workshop and headed for the
Barnaby wing, Poppy and Jack flashed into action.

"Let's go," said Jack, jumping out of the cart.

They made sure everyone was back inside the Barnaby
Wing, and Poppy ran to turn on the Jukebox before hiding
again.

"What's that?" they heard Mordane say. "Soren, Morgrim,
go check it out... And on second thoughts, stay out there
and keep watch... We don't need any surprise visitors
tonight."

Soren and Morgrim walked back into the main Workshop,
heading to the Jukebox, their eyes cautiously scanning their
surroundings with every step.

Poppy and Jack stayed well hidden, holding their breath as
the elves turned the Jukebox off.

"Anything?" Mordane echoed from the other room.

"All fine. Jukebox turned itself on, that's all; must be on a
motion sensor thing," they yelled back.

She turned to the elf next to her and lowered her voice,
"Let's just turn it off," she said, unplugging it from the wall.

Satisfied that they were alone, the two elves walked around
the Workshop like a pair of bored toddlers, picking things
up, poking at them, and putting them down where they
didn't belong. It was making Poppy so mad, but she bided
her time, and finally, the elves were walking towards the
doors to check outside.

"Now!" said Jack.

With that, Poppy pulled the ribbon in her hand, connected
to the lid of a huge crate in the elves' path, releasing
hundreds of tiny baubles on the floor.

The first elf slid, reaching out to grab the other one's arm,
but they were quick and dodged them. Instead, they caught
a rope hanging from above, and BOOM! A giant glitter
bomb exploded over both of them.

The first elf was buried under a mountain of shiny silver glitter as the other one tried to clear glitter from their eyes to run away. As they moved, they also slipped on the baubles and ended up in a tangled mess on the floor. Poppy and Jack immediately took advantage of the elves' dazed and glittery state, running in circles around them until they were completely tied up in ribbons and put super sticky tape over their mouths for good measure.

"What on earth are they doing out there?" They heard Mordane's frustrated voice shouting from the Barnaby Wing. "Ravenna, go and find out what they are playing at; we're trying to work in here."

Poppy and Jack quickly hid again as Ravenna entered the room. "What the heck...?" she said, running towards the two elves on the floor and directly into Poppy and Jack's next trap.

Super Sticky Tape placed across the walkway. She spotted it just before running into it, but she was going too fast. She raised her arms to shield herself, but it was too late. It worked perfectly; she was like a fly stuck on a spider's web. The more she struggled, the more stuck she became, and her muffled cries were barely noticeable. Poppy and Jack high-fived each other as they set their final trap and waited patiently for their next victim.

They had expected Mordane to send Kalethorn out to see where Ravenna had gone, but he didn't appear.

"We're going to have to draw him out," said Jack.

Poppy nodded, "I've got an idea," she said. "Follow me." They headed over to a workbench that she'd noticed earlier. It was full of toy cars and trucks, and Jack immediately saw what Poppy had in mind.

"Genius," he grinned.

It was a huge remote-controlled tank complete with a missile launcher. "Go make a couple of snowballs," Poppy said as Jack ran outside.

The Opposers watched their every move, desperately trying to break free and warn the others.

Poppy and Jack loaded the missile launcher and rolled it down to the Barnaby Wing.

Once in position, Jack expertly drove it inside and at first, no one noticed; they were too deep in their discussion...

"You're absolutely sure this is all the gifts both of you?" Mordane was saying. "Because once we open the chest with Barnaby's magic, we won't have long to - What's that?" he said, looking curiously at the tank as Jack launched the first snowball straight at Kalethorn.

Elsie immediately understood what was happening, recognizing the plan to lure them out in small groups, and she played along.

"Soren!" she said, laughing. "Not funny!"

Jack launched another snowball at Kalethorn, this time hitting him directly in the face.

"Puh," he said, spitting bits of snow out of his mouth. "Is this your idea of a joke, you three?" He said furiously, marching out of the Barnaby Wing to confront them.

Poppy and Jack stayed completely still, hidden behind the door as he entered the tunnel.

"Think you're funny, do you?" he said, approaching the main Workshop. "I'll teach you to mess with me. I -"

He never finished his sentence, confused by something that had happened. He'd walked into something on the floor, some kind of wire. He looked up as a giant candy cane came swinging towards him, attaching itself to his belt and swinging him into the main Workshop, where he saw the other Opposers already captured.

Poppy and Jack ran back into the Workshop and hid as he looked at them bewildered, hanging from the ceiling.

"THAT'S ENOUGH!" they heard Mordane's voice thunder from the other room. "Enough of this ridiculous behaviour, all of you," the voice was getting closer and closer. "We have a job to do; have you forgotten that?" he screamed, his voice trailing off as he entered the Workshop and saw his team in various states of detainment.

"Who's here?" he said immediately, "Show yourself."

Poppy and Jack tried to stay hidden, but Kalethorn had a bird's eye view and had been watching them the whole time.

"There," he said, pointing in their direction. "There's two of them."

"Ah ha," said Mordane, walking over to them with an evil smile on his face. "And who is it that we have here?"

With nowhere left to hide, they stood up to face Mordane.

"I'm Poppy, and this is my brother, Jack," Poppy replied, a sense of fearlessness spreading over her.

"Well, Poppy and Jack, it certainly looks like you've been busy. To what do we owe the pleasure of your company tonight?" Mordane said sarcastically.

"We're here to save Christmas," said Jack, standing slightly taller.

Mordane smiled a curious smile. "Save Christmas, you say?" he said, sounding interested. "Well then, Jack, you and I are on the same team. That's all we want too, to save Christmas from this circus that it's become."

"No, you want to destroy Christmas," Jack said. "And we're here to stop you!"

Mordane chuckled loudly. "Stop us? My boy, you have no idea how deep this goes. You stop us tonight, and more of us turn up tomorrow, the next night, and the next night until this is done. You can't stop us," he hissed.

"It's over, Mordane," said Poppy. Mordane seemed shocked that she knew his name but quickly regained his composure.

"Dear, sweet Poppy... it's only over when I say it's over," he said, his lips curling. "And mark my words, this is just the start."

The other Opposers sneered in the background; they thought they were so clever.

"YuleTrek has the others captured at the Snow Ball," Jack revealed.

Mordane's face flashed with anger before returning to normal. "Darrian, Bramma, Morgana, Thorne...I guess it's been a while since you heard from them?" Jack taunted Mordane.

"Oh well, I guess you got us then; we'd better head home," Mordane said.

Poppy could tell he still thought he had the upper hand, and she felt more determined than ever to bring him down. "But it's not just them, is it?" she said. "We know about the other Opposers too...the ones undercover."

This time, Mordane couldn't hide his emotions. He was visibly boiling with anger, which only spurred Poppy on more. "Westley from the Workshop, who helped you get in here tonight, Molly from YuleTrek, who messed with the routes yesterday, they're all detained at the Snow Ball," she announced.

There was still hope on Mordane's face as he remembered one Opposer who wasn't at the Snow Ball tonight, but Jack picked up on it right away.

"Wait, Poppy, you are forgetting someone ... Elara, she wasn't at the Snow Ball tonight. The team had to make a special trip to Barnaby's cabin to find her. We didn't want anyone feeling left out." he said, smiling at Mordane.

Mordane was silent; he knew the game was up. His eyes darted towards the exit, and he started to run.

"What about us?" screamed the other Opposers, but Mordane pretended not to hear them. He kept running towards the doors, picking up speed at an alarming rate.

"Oh, no, you don't," Jack said, pulling out the Tinsel Twirler Five Hundred from Wren's bag and firing it at Mordane. A thin strip of tinsel shot out and expanded mid-air into a thick, bushy bundle that wrapped itself around Mordane again and again, until you could barely see his face.

"Elsie, untie me!" he demanded, spitting bits of tinsel out of his mouth.

"I'm sorry, Mordane, but I swore to protect Christmas from being destroyed...I just didn't realize until it was too late that I picked the wrong side." Elsie said, smiling at Poppy and Jack.

This was the final straw for Mordane, who started screaming in rage.

Suddenly, the Workshop door burst open. "Blimey, someone's got their tree lights in a tangle! What's all the fuss about?" Poppy instantly recognized the voice.

It was Wren! Followed by Giselle, Santa, and the rest of the Yule Trek and Workshop elves.

They paused momentarily, looking at the chaos and the sprawl of tied-up Opposers across the Workshop. Then Wren smiled a smile so bright, it lit up the whole room. "I knew you could do it!" he said, beaming, rushing over with Giselle to hug Poppy and Jack.

"I see the Tinsel Twirler came in handy," he winked, looking at the Mordane-shaped pile of tinsel on the floor.

"Oh, well done, both of you," Giselle said with a huge smile. "Are you both okay?" She didn't wait for an answer; she just hugged them tightly again as Santa approached the group.

Poppy couldn't believe that this was how they were meeting Santa. It was so strange to see him in his formal Snow Ball attire instead of his usual red suit.

Tonight, he wore a dark green suit with golden trim and a gold buckle on his belt, but despite the victory against The Opposers, Santa looked troubled. The day's events had clearly taken their toll on him.

With a heart full of gratitude, Santa shook their hands in appreciation. "Poppy and Jack, the North Pole owes you a great debt. Thank you for everything you've done for us tonight. Your story will live in the hearts of the North Pole for a very long time," he said, his face filled with thanks.

Poppy couldn't find the right words, but she gave Santa a huge smile.

"It was our pleasure, Santa," Jack said as he shook his hand.

Santa thanked them one last time and then turned his attention to The Opposers, especially Mordane.

"I'm truly sorry we couldn't find a way to all live together in peace. It saddens me that your hearts have been filled with such needless hatred all this time. But treason against the North Pole and your fellow elves is unforgivable. Shame on you all." The Opposers didn't look ashamed; they looked angry and bitter. "Let's get them outside with the others," Santa instructed as the Yule Trek and Workshop teams started releasing The Opposers.

Santa turned to Elsie. "Miss Shadowthorn, I'd like to talk to you, please." Everyone else, we'll meet you outside." Poppy wished she could be a fly on the wall for that conversation, but Wren was ushering them outside at an unusually fast pace. "Wait till you see it," he said. "It's unbelievable."

- CHAPTER SEVENTEEN -

BANISHED

Lined up outside were the rest of The Opposers from the Snow Ball, and stood behind them, shimmering in the night sky were ten fully grown Aurora Wolves and their cubs.

"Can you believe it?" said Wren, looking utterly mesmerised by their presence.

"Where did they come from?" asked Poppy, shocked to see so many of the wolves.

"It's quite a story," he said. "Let me start at the beginning; as you know, Giselle created her distraction at the Snow Ball."

"What was the distraction?" Jack blurted out, his excitement getting the best of him.

"Oh, it was amazing; tell them Giselle"

Giselle beamed. "I started a balloon fight with some of the younger elves. I knew if I could get some balloons near the chandelier, they would heat up and burst, but it worked even better than I expected. The sound was incredible!"

"Genius!" Jack said, impressed.

"Well, actually, I have you to thank, Jack. I was inspired by what you did, using the children to create a distraction," Giselle said. "The Opposers are too arrogant to consider children a threat; it was perfect."

"How did you get them to pop at the right time?" Poppy asked curiously.

Giselle pulled a paper straw out of her pocket.

"With this," she said. "They make excellent pea shooters! I hit the first balloon, and it set off a chain reaction. I think it scared some of the older elves, though; they weren't too happy with me," she added regretfully.

"They'll get over it," said Wren. "Once they know how it helped save the North Pole. We might need Rufus's help to convince some of them, though," he chuckled.

"Sorry, Wren," Jack said, realising he had interrupted Wren's original story. "So, what happened after the distraction?"

Wren was looking around for someone. "Ah, Mohan!" he shouted, spotting him across the street and gesturing for him to come over. "Do you have a moment to tell Poppy and Jack about the cabin? They have to hear it from the man himself."

Mohan still looked like he could barely believe it himself, but he did his best to explain. "So, after Giselle created the distraction, I used a portal to get to Barnaby's cabin. I could see Elara inside; she was on the radio with other Opposers, giving them the final update. I don't know how, but afterwards, she must have spotted me and slipped out into the forest. I searched and searched, and I was just about to give up and call the others when I saw a huge flash of light and a whole pack of Aurora Wolves coming out from the trees. It was so unbelievable that I didn't notice at first, but the largest one had Elara in its mouth; she must have fainted from shock when she saw them coming after her. They must've been close by and sensed she was a threat to the North Pole."

Wren looked amazed like it was the first time he was hearing the story. "Tell them how you ended up here," he encouraged Mohan.

"Well, I didn't know what to do. We know so little about Aurora Wolves, except for the songs we used to sing at school, and as you know, until yesterday, we thought they were extinct. I didn't have anything to offer them like you guys did, so I raised my hands to show them I meant no harm. One of the females approached me and locked eyes with me for ages, and eventually, she lifted her tail and waved it at me just like Wren said happened to you guys. Then she laid down on the ground like she wanted me to climb on her back, so I did, and they brought us back into town. At first, I wasn't sure if they knew where they were going, but as soon as we entered the North Pole, they sniffed out the other Opposers at the Snow Ball and brought us here."

Poppy gazed at the wolves in amazement. It was a remarkable sight to see them all lined up like this.

"What do you think they want?" asked Jack.

"To fulfil their duty, the task they were born to do," Giselle said, smiling and looking at Wren.

"You know, I couldn't remember the song yesterday?" They nodded. "Well, I looked it up after what you said earlier, Poppy."

"With coats that shimmer of Northern Lights.
Guardians of the Arctic Nights,
If your heart holds no harm, they'll stand by your side,
But if you pose a threat, then there's nowhere to hide.
Once you've faced their spectral eyes,
In their protection, you'll forever reside.

When threat is near, their numbers grow,
Protecting the North from fiendish foe.
Those who seek to cause us pain will forever feel their watchful
reign."

"So they will watch over The Opposers and make sure they don't return?" asked Poppy.

Wren nodded. "But where will they go?" Jack wondered.

"They'll go to the outer borders," Mohan explained. "We'll build more cabins for them to live there, but they won't ever set foot in the North Pole again." His voice trailed off as Santa and Elsie finally came out of the Workshop.

Elsie looked out at the long line of Opposers in front of her, who were booing and jeering at her while the wolves howled in response to Santa's arrival. The history in their blood, responding to him as the purest embodiment of the North Pole and the leader of their pack.

"It's not every day you find out you're the leader of an ancient Wolfpack, is it?" Wren grinned. "That noise is going to take some getting used to!"

Santa approached the wolves and spoke in the same strange language that Elsie used when she opened the underground chamber to Barnaby's magic earlier.

"What language is that?" Poppy asked Giselle.

"Polarian," she replied. "It's the ancient language of the elders." Santa finished what he was saying and walked back towards the Workshop. The Wolves respectfully bowed to him and set off into the night with The Opposers as the Workshop and YuleTrek elves cheered. Poppy walked over to Elsie, who hadn't spoken since stepping outside with Santa.

"Are you okay?" she asked her.

Elsie nodded, appreciating her concern. "Santa has agreed to let me stay in the North Pole," she said. She raised her voice, addressing everyone in the crowd. "To everyone here, I want to say that I am so sorry. I don't expect your forgiveness, but please know I will do everything possible to make things up to you."

She looked around at Wren, Giselle, Mohan, and the other elves from YuleTrek and the Workshop. None of them seemed quite ready to accept her apology yet.

"Thank you, Elsie. I'm sure everyone appreciates that; there will be plenty of time to talk in the coming weeks," said Santa. "But for now, we have what's left of a Snow Ball to enjoy and Christmas to prepare for!" he declared as everyone cheered.

Jack suddenly looked sad.

"What's wrong?" asked Poppy, confused by his sudden change of mood.

"It's what Santa said about preparing for Christmas, it made me think of Mum and Dad, that's all," he said.

She smiled. "Don't worry, we'll be back soon."

Giselle and Wren stopped celebrating with the other elves and looked at each other. Poppy could tell something was wrong.

"What's going on?" she asked.

Wren and Giselle looked mortified.

"With everything that's happened today, we haven't been able to build the portal to get you home," said Wren, his voice filled with regret.

"Okay?" said Jack, not really seeing the problem. "That's alright, we can build it tomorrow, can't we?"

Wren was beside himself, unable to speak, so Giselle took over. "Do you remember me saying there were limitations on the time tunnel portals? That they had to be used 'between two relatively close periods of time.'" Poppy started to understand what they were trying to say, and she felt sick.

"We've gone past the time when we can return you to before you went missing," Giselle continued, sounding just as upset as Wren.

"I'm so sorry," Wren blurted out. "If I hadn't taken us to the carnival yesterday and had gotten on with the portal like I was supposed to, none of this would have happened." He was inconsolable, feeling so guilty for letting his friends down.

They hated to see him so upset. "If you hadn't taken us to the carnival, there wouldn't be a Christmas to go home to," Jack said kindly.

"Yes," said Poppy, fully agreeing with Jack that no one was to blame here. They were just as guilty of wanting to go to the carnival. "Wren, please don't get upset. None of us could have predicted what was going to happen today."

Poppy wasn't angry with Wren or anyone for that matter, but the thought of returning home to the present time where her parents had spent all this time thinking that they were missing was unbearable.

"What about the Christmas Eve portals?" Jack said, trying to find a solution. "Couldn't we use one of those?"

"It won't work," said Wren. "Those portals were made some days ago to specific locations. They're only set to go back a few hours here and there to help Santa deliver everyone's gifts."

Elsie had been watching the conversation from the steps. "I think I can help you," she said as they all looked at her. Wren and Giselle seemed suspicious, but Poppy and Jack were keen to hear what she had to say.

"I think with Barnaby's magic, I can give a little boost to the Chrono Quartz to still get you home before you went missing," she said.

Poppy was overcome with emotion; her body took over, and she unexpectedly ran up to Elsie and hugged her.

Elsie was completely taken aback, and Poppy realised that there probably wasn't much hugging that went on in the hateful community she was from.

Instead of backing off, this made her hug Elsie even tighter as Elsie began to hug her back, realising that she needed a hug as much as Poppy did tonight.

Poppy let go, and Elsie went to say something else. "I've actually been thinking about something else I'd like to do with the magic with your support," she said to everyone. They all looked at her, curious to know what she would say next, Santa included.

"I want to fulfil Barnaby's wishes," she said.

"His real wishes," she added quickly as she saw the elves' worried expressions. "Barnaby had been working on an idea at his cabin all those years ago. I found the plans in his diary. He wanted to create 'The Bells of Blessing'. His intention was that the sound of the bells would remind each of us that Christmas is a time to count the blessings we have and not only focus on what we are about to receive. He had plans to make this the fourth item in The Enchanted Trinity... I suppose making it 'The Enchanted Quartet,'" she smiled.

The elves and Santa were moved by this beautiful idea. "It's perfect!" said Santa, his voice overwhelmed with emotion for his dear friend. "We'll make space in the Barnaby Wing for the new 'Enchanted Quartet!'" he declared.

Elsie looked at him and smiled. "Actually, Santa... Barnaby had a different intention for the bells," she said. Everyone looked at her, curious to understand what she meant. "The Bells of Blessing are for your sleigh," she said, her voice filled with pride for this incredible idea from her ancestor. "It's written that the sound of the bells, jingling in the night sky, shall fill the hearts of all who hear them with the true spirit of Christmas."

Santa's face was a mixture of sadness and admiration. "Beautiful," he said. "I only wish he had been able to tell me himself."

Gathering himself, Santa had a final announcement to make to everyone.

"By my calculations, this means that we have the rest of the night to enjoy the Snow Ball together, and tomorrow, Poppy and Jack, we'll get you home."

They headed back to the Snow Ball, their hearts fuller than ever of Christmas Spirit. They danced, sang and celebrated, sharing the timeless traditions of the elves and Christmas with one another.

Later, Santa sat in his armchair and told tales of him and Barnaby as young men and new stories of the Bells of Blessing.

It was a perfect night.

Exhausted, yet somehow fuller of energy than she'd ever felt, Poppy fell into bed that night at Giselle's, feeling incredibly grateful.

- CHAPTER EIGHTEEN -

HOMEWARD BOUND

"Hurry up, Jack, we don't want to be late," Giselle said, gently guiding him out of the kitchen as he devoured one last pancake.

"I'm going to miss these," he said fondly to Poppy. This morning, they'd skipped their shrinking potion, returning to their regular size. For Jack, that meant he needed four times the usual amount of breakfast.

They would meet Elsie and Wren at Santa's cottage, where Barnaby's magic had been kept safe last night. They rode the tram for one last time, but today was a new experience. Before, they'd been doing everything to blend in; now, they stuck out like sore thumbs. Not just because they were twice as big as everyone else on board but also because it seemed that there wasn't anyone in the North Pole who hadn't heard about their encounter with Mordane and The Opposers at the Workshop last night.

As they reached the tram stop, the elves burst into applause. Poppy felt embarrassed by the attention, but Jack revelled in the spotlight. Telling an increasingly exciting tale that made them sound like a couple of superheroes. Well-wishers and applause followed them throughout the North Pole, all the way to Santa's front door, where Wren had already arrived on his snowmobile.

Giselle took a moment to fix her hair and straighten her tunic before seeing Mrs Claus. In fact, she hadn't stopped talking about her all morning; Mrs Claus was her baking idol.

Wren was the first to spot them from the window and ran out. "Wow, I forgot how tall you are," he said as he approached them. "Come, come, everyone's inside."

The centrepiece of The Claus's living room was a large, crackling fireplace. A huge Christmas tree reaching to the ceiling stood in the corner decorated with delicate ornaments from all over the world.

In the opposite corner stood a mahogany grandfather clock. The pendulum had been crafted to look like a seesaw, with elves rocking back and forth and a charming miniature train wound around the whole clock, carrying gifts and twinkling lights.

"Giselle, how lovely to see you," said Mrs Claus. "Congratulations on the bake-off win yesterday; by the way, you were marvellous." "Giselle looked positively star-struck.

She welcomed Poppy and Jack and thanked them for everything they had done for the North Pole.

Poppy had always pictured Mrs Claus as an elderly-looking woman with half-moon glasses, but actually, she didn't look that elderly at all. With silvery white hair, no glasses, and ruby red lipstick. She wore a fluffy white cape with a red and gold dress; there was an air of elegance and kindness about her.

Jack was looking at a certificate on the wall. "You're a vet?" he asked Mrs Claus.

"Yes, that's right," she said. "Someone round here's got to keep an eye on how much icing sugar Rudolph is eating!"

She looked over at Santa, who looked guilty of perhaps spoiling Rudolph with his favourite treats too often.

"That's actually how I met Santa; I was training when he travelled the globe, spreading the word about Christmas."

"Have you ever worked with Wolves?" Poppy asked, thinking about the new additions to the North Pole.

"Not yet," Mrs. Claus chuckled. "But I'm ready to learn, and if they need anything, I'll be here."

She poured them each a cup of hot chocolate and put a plate of cookies down as they sat by the fire to discuss the plan.

When they were ready, Elsie placed Barnaby's chest on top of the coffee table and opened it with a small silver key.

It was like a thousand tiny sparklers had been set alight. Elsie quickly directed some of the sparks towards the portal to give the Chrono Quartz a boost. Then she started speaking in Polarian, reading from Barnaby's diary.

Shimmering sparks danced and weaved through the air, forming elaborate patterns, and then went away as the chest closed sharply behind them.

A few moments later, Elsie opened it again, and an incredibly bright light burst from within, leaving behind a single set of bells.

As she picked them up, they jingled, a sound so beautiful and cheerful that Poppy's heart felt like it had been set on fire.

Elsie passed them to Santa, who looked at them carefully before wrapping them in a blanket to attach to his sleigh later.

"That was amazing," said Jack. "That sound was wonderful; well done, Elsie." She smiled at him.

The room went silent; they were all filled with different emotions today. The bells of blessing, leaving the North Pole, the excitement of seeing their parents. It was confusing to feel happy and sad at the same time.

Giselle and Wren kept looking at them, knowing that their time together was coming to an end. Giselle came over with tears in her eyes.

"Stay in touch, won't you? You can write to the North Pole anytime. We want to hear all about the rest of your trip and Christmas at your grandparents," she said as Mrs Claus handed her a tissue.

Wren came over next to say goodbye, "Don't forget us, will you. Make sure you keep the Christmas spirit alive out there," he said. "We're going to miss you so much." He walked towards the window at the back of the room. "In fact, there were a few others that wanted to say a proper goodbye," he opened the curtains, and there, grazing on hay in the garden next to Santa's sleigh, were the reindeer!

"Santa brought them over to see you off," he said.

They couldn't believe it. They hugged Santa and ran outside to see them. Apart from Giselle and Wren, the reindeer were what Poppy would miss the most about the North Pole.

When they returned inside, Santa had some final words to say.

"Poppy and Jack, it doesn't bear thinking about how things would have turned out yesterday if you hadn't been here with us. The North Pole will never forget what you did for us." He walked towards another chest on top of the fireplace and took something out.

"Jack, this is a snow globe that was given to me by Barnaby when I first left the North Pole. To anyone else, it looks like a regular snow globe, but for you and Poppy, when you shake it and ask, you can see anything in the North Pole so that you will always remember your time here."

Jack looked honoured; he instantly shook it and asked to see the Workshop. Sure enough, the Snow Globe responded and showed him the team making their final preparations for Christmas.

Santa returned to the chest and took out a second item, handing it to Poppy.

"For you, Poppy, my compass. Just like the snow globe, to anyone else, it will be useless, but for you and Jack, it will always point you in the direction of the North Pole in case you ever need to find your way back."

They were gifts they would treasure forever.

They hugged everyone one last time before dropping the portal around them.

They landed in their beds at the hotel.

If everything had gone to plan, it should have been the morning of the dog sledding, and suddenly, they heard their mother's voice. "Poppy! Jack! Come to our room when you're ready. We've ordered breakfast here to save time; it won't be long."

They beamed at each other and ran into the other room as fast as their legs could carry them, hugging their parents so tightly that Poppy thought she might never let go. "Good morning! Nice to see you too!" Mr Brown said, laughing. "Are you two feeling ok?"

"Fine," said Poppy. "Just excited to be here with you, that's all," she smiled.

There was a knock on the door, and soon, they were enjoying a perfect family breakfast again.

After they were done, they went to get ready, and Poppy pretended she wasn't feeling too great.

"Is there any chance we can skip the dog sledding today?" she asked.

Mrs Brown checked her over, and even though she couldn't find anything wrong with her, they decided to stay at the hotel and play games by the fire today. Mr Brown would rearrange the dog sledding for another day.

"I'm really sorry, mum and dad," she said later.

"No need to apologise," said Mr Brown. "All that matters on this trip is spending time together." She hugged him tightly. He had no idea how right he was.

A few days later, after an amazing trip in Greenland, the Brown family flew home to London and spent a magical Christmas Day in Norfolk at their Grandparent's house. Poppy and Jack would always remember their time at the North Pole and the legends of the elves who lived there. They'd learnt so much from them, just like Santa himself.

Meanwhile, in the North Pole on Christmas day, Giselle found a special envelope under her tree.

Dear Giselle and Wren,

Merry Christmas!

We tracked down the chef at our hotel, and he gave us the recipe for Kalaallit Kaagiat for you - We hope you like it better than we did! We told our parents that we have some new pen-friends from Greenland, so please write back anytime and keep us posted with everything going on in the North Pole.
Say hello to the reindeer for us. We're always checking in on them using Jack's snow globe.
Thanks again for everything you did for us. We had the best Christmas ever!
Hope to hear from you both soon. If you need it, Santa has our address (Bad joke alert from Jack)

Poppy and Jack

Giselle was touched by their gift. She whipped up Kalaallit Kaagiat for Christmas Day dessert, only to discover that they didn't like it either, which she and Wren found utterly hilarious.

Even though the recipe didn't work out, their quest for it had introduced them to many other things they'd always cherish: new friendships and unforgettable memories. Even if the North Pole wasn't quite ready to give up sugar, one thing was for sure – they'd never give up on Christmas spirit...

The Christmas season came and went,
Foes were vanquished, banished, and spent.
The elves began preparations anew,
For next year's Christmas, its spirit so true.
In every heart, bells of blessing did chime,
Rekindling the magic of this enchanting time.
Under snow and stars, where dreams take flight,
The elves of the Arctic kept Christmas alight.

Printed in Great Britain
by Amazon